The Legend of Amanda Robins

Corrine Annette Zahra

First published in 2014 by
FARAXA
faraxapublishing.com / faraxabooks.com
info@faraxapublishing.com

The Legend of Amanda Robins

Published by
FARAXA Publishing
38 Antonio Nani Street, Rabat RBT 3047, Malta; and
P. O. Box 37, East Longmeadow, MA 01020, USA.
http://faraxapublishing.com
info@faraxapublishing.com

ISBN 978-0-9893028-9-0

Printed in the United States of America.

DEDICATION

To my grandfather, Coronato Portelli.
May he rest in peace for eternity.

ACKNOWLEDGMENTS

I would like to thank my dad for the commitment he gave me, for helping me as a "manager" and for all the nights we watched movies together, which gave me the idea to write
The Legend of Amanda Robins.

I would also like to thank Joanne Micallef, founder and director of FARAXA Publishing, for helping me turn the story of Amanda into a published book, making it available to the public worldwide.

CONTENTS

Foreward

The Legend of Amanda Robins by Corrine Zahra is a fast-moving, gripping account of the turmoil resulting from the destruction of Magic State, an invisible island north of Australia. Queen Amanda is forced to evacuate her land and send the inhabitants to live with humankind. Her ex-husband, Dylan, has escaped from a prison island with hoards of werewolves and launched a vicious attack. She herself goes to New York where she works in a supermarket and meets Logan, her new husband-to-be.

This fantasy tale reaches deep into the imagination of this young author who never disappoints with her inventiveness. From the streets of New York, where new Twin Towers are born, to the White House and a press conference with Barack Obama, Queen Amanda puts all her powers on display. War and intrigue permeate the pages of Ms Zahra's book which should prove un-put-downable for lovers of magical creatures.

My recent connection with the dramatic work of Corrine Zahra warms me to her prose. Her play *Back in Time* had a successful showing and as much as I wish her success with her prose, I hope she will return to writing for the stage.

Rob Ricards

🦇 Chapter 1 🦇

Change for Amanda
(2004)

Amanda, for me, is real. She uncovers truth and power like no other known person in the world. May I tell you this story. You might not believe it, but it is true.

Amanda was upset to discover that her husband, Dylan, was tricking her throughout all this time, to kill her and take her crown. Now, you are probably wondering what this crown stuff is all about. Truth is, Amanda is the queen of Magic State – an island north of Australia. However, you cannot see this island on which magical creatures live. Fairies, wizards, warlocks, vampires, werewolves, leprechauns, unicorns, pixies and so on. Amanda was originally a vampire. Your parents say that such creatures do not exist but, trust me, they do and Amanda was queen of them all. You might think these magical creatures could hurt you, but they do not. They are as good as chocolate. Amanda was part of the Robins family which was entrusted with the power to rule Magic State only for good being. It is a good idea that you meet Dylan to understand the whole story.

~ ~ ~ ~ ~

A few months before, everything was perfect in Magic State. The magical creatures lived in harmony. Amanda was at a meeting with the mayors of each town, all of whom were reporting news of their towns.

"I think it's a good idea that we build a new university in San Magisco. Students need more education and it would make San Magisco more popular with others," said the mayor of San Magisco, Neil Huntanur.

"All who agree with this say 'Aye,'" said the mayor of Fantasy City, Roberta Lamustrai.

From the courtroom, only a quarter of the mayors said aye.

"I do not agree, it's a waste. We have two universities which are enough for our country," said Amanda in a demanding tone.

Neil Huntanur had a very angry expression on his face: "Your Highness . . ."

Amanda cut him off.

"It will be a waste to build another, Huntanur," she said.

There was silence and everyone was looking at Huntanur to see what he was going to say.

"Your Highness, what is that?" Roberta said.

Amanda looked towards where Roberta was pointing. From the window, it appeared as though there was a huge, black cloud. *That's not a cloud,* thought Amanda. Instantly, she knew what it was. Amanda stood up from her seat.

"Everyone, go back to your towns and make sure that you evacuate everyone to Atlantis," she bellowed.

"Why? What's going on?" a mayor asked.

"They've escaped," replied Amanda, her face turning whiter than ever.

"It cannot be! The MCST (Magical Creatures Squad Team) is supposed to be guarding the prison!" another mayor exclaimed.

"Well, they've escaped. They've all escaped from Evil Spirit. Now, everyone, go do as I said," Amanda yelled.

All present went running to inform the people, while Amanda sat down on her throne. Evil Spirit was an island on the other end of the world; far, far away from Magic State. However, it was not only an island, but also a prison.

The filthy man is coming back, now, to destroy what I've been working so hard for. He did tell me and I didn't listen. I'm going to kill him. That horrible ex-husband of mine, Amanda thought. She sprinted from where she was and informed the whole castle.

"What now, mom?" asked Cindy, her daughter.

"We fight," replied Amanda.

Everyone in Magic State was waiting for death. So many prisoners from Evil Spirit had escaped and now everyone was doomed. Amanda and the MCST stood waiting around the coasts of the island, ready to fight. Many had told Amanda to go to Atlantis, the magical sea land, for protection, but she refused. Amanda had to get rid of Dylan.

Once the escaped prisoners arrived, the war began. Gun shots and dead bodies. It was a scary place for all present. No one was braver than these people. Amanda was looking for Dylan, she wanted him dead.

From the sky, Amanda searched along the perimeter of the island as she could fly. Finally, she spotted

Dylan at Woodland – he was fighting against her best friend, Maria. Amanda flew straight down to that spot with a thunderous look on her face.

"Hello, Amanda," Dylan said, with a wide smile on his face.

"You, little . . ." she started.

Amanda punched Dylan in the face. He smiled back at her, looking drunk.

"Maria, go! I'll take care of him," said Amanda, imperiously.

Maria nodded and left.

"You're dead!" Dylan snarled.

The fight between them began.

Amanda swung and Dylan punched back. Amanda was furious. She wanted him to experience great pain. Dylan noticed that he had little to no chance against Amanda. He ran towards the forest. Amanda followed.

Amanda ran towards Dylan with vampire speed, but he was similarly fast as he was a werewolf. Amanda kept knocking down trees in his path, to block him, but he was clever and always got out of the way.

Dylan then knocked down a branch and Amanda got stuck beneath it. She forced the branch off her and ran with all her might towards Dylan. She wanted so badly to bite him in the neck. He stopped suddenly and turned back into human form.

"Tired?" he asked with a devious grin.

"Not one, little bit," Amanda retorted.

She sprinted towards Dylan and grabbed his neck, then held him up and pinned him with all her strength to an old oak tree.

"You're going to die! Any last words?" threatened Amanda.

Dylan smiled cunningly and scratched Amanda on the cheek with his claw. Instead of healing, the cut started growing larger. Amanda felt like her whole body was melting. She let go of Dylan and crumpled to the floor . . .

~ ~ ~ ~ ~

Amanda did not die. For a second, that is what you thought, right? No, she did not die. She was poisoned.

A werewolf could create enough venom to kill any human or magical being. Amanda would have died if it was not for Maria who had seen the fight and went after her. Dylan escaped narrowly from being killed. Amanda was sent to the hospital in Woodland and cured.

The war lasted for three weeks and Amanda wanted to go searching for Dylan again. But he was nowhere to be found. Amanda was also very weak, so she let Maria take charge of everything while she stayed in hospital.

Maria sorted everything out and, within weeks, the prisoners were all hypnotized to stop fighting. Magic State was a mess. Many houses and buildings had been burned down to ashes. It was a horrible sight. Not many people died, which was good news. Of course, the prisoners who had escaped were sent back to Evil Spirit, to rot in prison.

Amanda was still not herself, so Maria and Amanda's children, Cindy and Max, took charge. Maria decided to bring the prisoners back from Evil Spirit, to rebuild Magic State and restore the whole country to its glory. Many people were homeless and Amanda decided to do what she hated the most, to safeguard her people. She announced that the whole country needed to go and live with humans, in their countries, to be safe. Many were against this but Amanda had no choice, otherwise the people would starve and die. Amanda herself was forced to move in with humans, given her trust in the MCST. It turned out that the guards in Evil Spirit had been knocked out, which is why the prisoners had escaped. But now, they were all hypnotized to rebuild Magic State, by day and by night. Dylan himself was sent to Evil Spirit for eternity . . .

~ ~ ~ ~ ~

Now you know how much pain Dylan caused Amanda. The worst part was that her land was destroyed, but her people, at least, were safe. Amanda went to live in New York City with her parents and her children, Cindy and Max. Maria also went along. Amanda healed and returned to normal, but she was also in so much grief over what had happened in Magic State, that she stayed mostly quiet throughout the days.

Cindy and Max became sick of seeing their mother like this. Cindy was 17 years old, with brown straight hair, whereas Max was 18 years old and had curly, red hair like his mom. Both Cindy and Max had their mother's eyes: green. Amanda was not crying, but she was not herself.

"Mom, please stop this. I'm tired and sick of you being so, what's the word?" said Max.

"Glum," replied Cindy. "Max, for once, is right. You shouldn't do this to yourself."

Cindy was also a vampire, but she liked helping. She was tidy, unlike her older brother who was a slob, sorry to say. The reason for his slobbishness was because he was a werewolf.

"Hey!" said Max, glaring at his sister.

"Don't worry about dad, he's been sent to Evil Spirit. And, soon, Magic State will be rebuilt and ready for us to move back in."

"Mom, are you even hearing us?" Cindy asked.

"Can you both shut up? I'm tired of hearing you tell me to get over it. It's not easy. All I want is to go back to Magic State and take charge. But, no! We're stuck here in New York City, waiting for the darn prisoners to rebuild the towns they destroyed. So, please, shut up and leave me alone!" Amanda yelled, storming upstairs to her study.

"What just happened?" said Julia – Amanda's mother.

"I think mom's angry," said Max.

"I think it's better to let her cool off," replied Julia.

She went into the laundry room to continue her chores.

Amanda was in her study. Her green eyes scanned the

walls. She was looking at all the newspapers of *The Magic State Times* as they hung there, on those walls. Those were the golden days.

Amanda was living in New York City because, a few months ago, the First Magical War had taken place. Every magical creature ended up having to live among humans until the island returned to normal, since homes had been destroyed. As Amanda looked up at the walls in her room, a tear fell from her eye. But she was going to be strong. Amanda greatly missed Magic State. Who knew when she would be able to take her place on the throne?

Someone opened the door. Amanda turned around and saw that it was her father, Tony. He too had brown hair, but Amanda had inherited her red hair from her mother. Tony walked in and closed the door.

"Listen, my daisy duck, I know you're sad. But the day will come when you will rule again. You'll see all your people happy once more, but you have to wait for that time to come. Right now, we must be brave and hope for the best, not be glum. One day, we won't have to wear these horrible clothes humans wear. Don't worry, that day will come. Then we'll rise," said Tony, sitting down next to Amanda on the small couch.

He placed his hand on Amanda's shoulder and gave her a kiss on the forehead. Amanda smiled.

"Thanks, dad," she said, wiping her nose. "You kind of cheered me up."

"Good," replied Tony. "I've a proposal for you. Would you like to go bowling tonight? I know, it's different from the way we play it, but it's close."

Amanda noticed that her father was only trying to cheer her up and she did not want him to think that she did not appreciate his offer. She accepted.

"Okay, I'll go."

"We'll all go," replied Tony.

By eight o'clock in the evening, the Robins family had eaten dinner and were preparing themselves to go bowling. Amanda did not really wish to go, but pretended to be happy for her father's sake. She still called him 'dad' even though she was 48 years old – a grown woman. But for Amanda, it was as though she was 20 years old, because magical creatures never grow old.

When the family arrived at the bowling alley, they rented their shoes and went to put them on. Maria sat down next to Amanda. She was her best friend.

"You don't really want to be here, do you?" Maria asked.

"Does it really show?" Amanda replied.

Maria was not just Amanda's best friend, but also her trusted advisor. When Maria was young, her parents had died in a car accident in Magic State. Tony and Julia had loved Maria as one of their own and adopted her. Ever since, Maria had been treated like one of the royal family. She was also a vampire.

"Yes. Don't worry, I won't tell," said Maria, smiling.

Amanda smiled in return. That was Maria. They got up to start playing. Game after game, Amanda was enjoying herself.

"You see how much fun you're having?" asked Tony. "You're right. Thanks," replied Amanda.

The family continued playing and all were having a great time. It was getting late and they had to go home. The house the Robins family was living in was not large. It was a 'normal' house which everyone hated, especially Amanda. Never in her life had she lived in such a small place! She had been raised in a palace.

The next day, Amanda and Maria went to find new jobs. Their last one had not really ended well. Tony went to work, while Julia stayed at home cleaning. Amanda's kids went to school.

Amanda heard that a new supermarket was opening nearby, so she went to check it out with Maria. They walked into the supermarket and spoke with the store manager who was delighted for them to start working there. He told them what they needed to do. They were going to be cleaners, so they just had to dust and organize the shelves. It was okay. They were going to be paid well, so they took the jobs. The manager said they could start tomorrow. Amanda was not happy about this working thing, but she had to fit in with all this horrid, normal, human stuff. The next day came by quickly and both of them got ready for work.

Amanda and Maria walked into the supermarket, checked in, put on their uniforms and started cleaning. Once in a while, the manager would come and check on them.

"Excuse me, but where do you find the bread section?" someone asked Amanda.

Amanda turned around and stopped what she was doing. There, in front of her, was the most handsome man she had ever met. From his smell, Amanda noticed that he was a vampire.

"Over there, sir. May I ask, are you a vampire?"

The man was startled.

"No. Vampires don't exist," he said nervously.

Amanda knew he was lying.

"Don't worry. I'm Amanda Robins," she said, taking off her glove and holding out her hand.

At that moment, the man realized who she was.

"Amanda Robins! As in *the* Amanda Robins?" he asked.

Amanda smirked: "Yes."

"Nice to meet you, Your Highness," the man said. "Well, I'm not that Highness at the moment. I'm cleaning instead of ruling on a throne chair."

The man laughed.

"Mind my manners! I'm Logan of the Lost," he said.

"Nice to meet you, too. How are things going?" asked Amanda.

"Fine. Our community's doing okay. Could be better of course, but fine," he replied.

Amanda smiled.

"I must be on my way, Your Highness. Hope to see you again," said Logan.

"Of course. Goodbye."

Logan walked off.

"He was cute," Maria said.

"Were you spying?" asked Amanda.

"Maybe. Maybe not."

They both started laughing. Amanda thought Logan was cute, but there was no way she would ever imagine herself with him. *I guess this human air might be doing me well,* she thought and continued her work.

Amanda could not stop thinking about Logan over the next few days. Meanwhile, Logan visited her daily. He also spoke with Maria, but the latter knew that his mind was full attention towards her friend. Amanda learned that Logan was from Woodland, loved to play golf with gnomes, was not married and loved politics.

All Amanda's problems were fading away. Tony and Julia were happy for their daughter – she was finally relaxing and taking a break from herself. Finally, Monday arrived. Logan walked into the supermarket. Amanda pretended not to notice him and continued working.

"Hello," said Logan.

"Hello to you," said Amanda. "How are you today?"

"Good. I have to make this quick as I'll be late for work. I was wondering if you'd like to catch a movie, sometime?" he said.

Amanda was startled. She never thought Logan would ask her something like that.

"What do you think? Too early?" he added.

"No. Perfect timing. Sure, I'll go see a movie with you," replied Amanda.

They decided on a time and day, then Logan left.

"Amanda likes Logan. Amanda likes Logan!" Maria said, the instant Logan was out of earshot.

"Stop it!" retorted Amanda.

"Hey! It's not my fault you like him," Maria smirked.

Amanda blushed.

"If you like him, act normal, not all queen-like. Be yourself," added Maria.

"Thanks," replied Amanda as they continued working.

Amanda could not wait until that evening. She skipped all the way home, while Maria made weird faces. Never in her whole life had Maria seen Amanda skip. She was acting like a kid. Amanda walked into the house, breathing in the fresh air and smiling widely. Cindy and Max started asking questions at the dinner table. Maria was totally freaking out.

At seven o'clock that evening, Logan picked Amanda up and they went to see a movie. Amanda wore normal clothes, but not too elegant, of course. They decided to watch *The Lone Ranger* – a hit comedy during which they could not stop laughing. After that night, Logan took Amanda out on a couple of more dates, as well. She liked spending time with him. One thing led to another and the pair started dating. Amanda was upset about the whole war and her beloved land being trashed, but Logan seemed to be the cure to it all. He had now become another open chapter in her life.

"Listen, Logan. I want you to come over for dinner tonight at my place," said Amanda.

They were at a coffee shop, obviously drinking coffee.

"Well, sure. I'd like to meet your parents," Logan told her.

Amanda started laughing. She felt like a teenager when he said that.

"Cindy and Max are going to be so excited. They really want a dad," Amanda replied.

Then she noticed what she had just said.

"Oh, really?! I didn't know we were getting married?" Logan joked.

Amanda felt embarrassed. Logan looked at his watch. "I've gotta go. See you tonight," Logan said and kissed her on the cheek.

"Bye," she replied.

"Bye."

Off he went.

Amanda was done working for the day and went home. She started cleaning. She wanted everything to be perfect for tonight. It was eight o'clock and Logan would soon be there.

"Don't put your feet on the coffee table!" Amanda yelled to Max. "And, Maria, stop walking around with that bacon in your pants!"

"Okay. It's just Logan, ya know?" replied Maria.

Amanda was seeing red.

"I'll be upstairs if you want me," Maria said, then ran upstairs.

At that moment, the bell rang. Amanda rushed to get it.

"Hey, Logan!"

"Hi, Amanda," Logan said, kissing her.

"Come on in," she replied.

Logan walked inside: "Nice place."

"Thanks," she answered.

"Hello. You must be Logan," Julia said, giving him a hug.

"Yeah. And you must be Julia," he replied.

"Yes, I am. It's nice to finally meet you. Come on in and feel like home," Julia replied and rushed to the kitchen. "I'm cooking pork. Hope you like it."

"I've never tried pork, but I'll have a go," he said.

"Let's sit down on the couch," suggested Amanda.

Logan and Amanda sat down.

"Didn't I tell you to put your feet down?" Amanda told Max who was sitting next to her.

Max glared at his mother and put his feet down, mumbling something.

"They're always like this," Amanda remarked.

Cindy ran through the living room at full speed towards the kitchen.

"I smell something good. Hmm," she said.

"Good," said Julia. "Go next to your mother, now."

Cindy walked into the living room.

"Hi, I'm Cindy. And you must be Logan," she said, sitting down on the couch.

"Hello. Nice to meet you," replied Logan. "Your mom talks a lot about you two."

Amanda blushed.

"Oh, really! Good or bad?" Cindy asked.

"So, so," Logan laughed.

"Well, I'm the good one. Max is everything else, including messy," said Cindy.

"I'm messy for a reason!' Max jumped in, defending his culture.

"What do you mean, messy?" Logan said.

"I'm a werewolf," said Max.

"Oh, really. First time I've heard this," Logan said, looking at Amanda.

She just shrugged. Amanda was going to kill her kids at any minute, now. The latter two started mimicking each other.

"May I ask," Logan whispered to Amanda, "how they don't drive you crazy?"

"I seriously don't know."

"Food's ready!" called out Julia.

Everyone rose to go to the dinner table. Even Maria came downstairs.

"Hi, Maria," Tony said.

"Hey," she replied.

"Where's your father?" Julia asked Amanda, as everyone sat down.

"I don't know," Amanda replied.

"Hmm, I smell food," said Tony, walking in.

He had oil all over his shirt.

"Tony, please be polite for once! We have a guest here," Julia said.

"Sorry."

Tony sat down on a chair.

"You're gonna change that shirt, right?" said Julia.

Tony got up and went to his room to change the shirt.

"Seriously, Logan," he said. "You're better off without 'em."

Logan smiled.

"Your dad must be a werewolf, as well?" he asked Amanda.

"Yes."

Julia served the food.

Tony came back with a much better shirt and they all started eating. Logan was really amazed with Julia's cooking.

"This is the best food I've had in days," he remarked.

Julia smiled: "Good thing."

When they had all finished eating, Maria and Julia washed the dishes, whereas the others went to the living room. Cindy and Max were still fighting. Amanda was going to lose her patience.

"So, tell me, Logan. What d'you do for a living?" Tony asked.

"Well, at the moment I'm an accountant," Logan answered.

"Good. In Magic State?" continued Tony.

"In Magic State, my family used to have a very popular bakery. Everyone used to come and buy from there," Logan said.

"Oh, that's good. So how's your family? Are they doing well, with the move and stuff?" Tony asked.

"Well, they're not here. They died."

"Logan, how come you never told me?" said Amanda.

"I don't like mentioning them," Logan said.

"I'm sorry I brought it up," replied Tony.

"It's okay," Logan said.

The rest of the night, Amanda was going to put a stake through her heart. She was quiet most of the time. She felt weird. She was the queen of Magic State and had a boyfriend. She was wearing these human clothes and totally freaking out. She still did not want to believe it . . .

Two Years Later

"Aww, Logan. You didn't need to do so much for me!" said Amanda.

Logan and Amanda were in a wonderful restaurant. Logan knew the owner and so paid him to make it a special occasion. It was their anniversary. They had been going out for two years, now. Amanda never wanted to believe it, so she always called it a dream. But, of course, this was reality.

The couple ordered their food and had a wonderful evening. It was around ten o'clock at night and Logan was about to tell Amanda something that was going to change her life forever.

"Amanda, I have to ask you something," he said.

"Oh, really? What?" she replied.

Amanda was excited. Logan knelt down, took out a small, velvet box and asked the words he had been repeating in his head for the last hour.

"Will you marry me?"

Opening the box, there was a beautiful ring that Logan wished would be Amanda's. Amanda was shocked. She put her hands over her mouth.

"Yes! A 100 times, yes!" she said and got up, hugging him.

Amanda knew she needed to think about her land, but it seemed that her worries were gone. All that mattered was Logan. Everyone was happy. Among the folks of Magic State, the news spread and everyone started preparing for the wedding.

With the words 'Yes, I do,' Amanda and Logan became husband and wife. No one could spoil that special day for them, not even Dylan . . .

⚡ Chapter 2 ⚡

Dylan is Back

Well, I hope you liked the first chapter of Amanda's life. But that was only the beginning. Now starts the story you might be looking for.

~ ~ ~ ~ ~

One morning, Amanda woke up and started making breakfast. She lived with her parents since Logan did not mind. They had been married for six months and everything was normal.

"Good morning, love dove," Logan said.

He had woken up because Amanda did. It was very weird, now, sleeping alone.

"Good morning," replied Amanda, planting him a kiss on the cheek. "Do you want eggs and bacon for breakfast?"

"Sure," replied Logan.

He sat down on a chair in the living room.

Amanda started to crack the eggs. It was April and spring was around the corner. The air was unusually fresh, even though this was New York where they were living. Amanda had gotten used to it there and loved it very much. The telephone started ringing and Amanda went to get it.

"Hello," she said.

No one answered. All she heard was breathing on the other end of the line, but Amanda was not scared one bit.

"Hello?" she asked again, with emphasis.

The person at the other end of the line hung up. Amanda was confused.

"Who was that?" said Logan.

"I don't know. Maybe, wrong number," she said.

Amanda continued making eggs and bacon for Logan. She was still wondering who the caller could have been. Maybe, it was an enemy of hers who had returned for revenge. As queen of Magic State, Amanda had a lot of enemies.

"Hey, mom," said Cindy, giving her a kiss on the cheek. "You're cooking bacon – my favorite!"

Cindy hugged Amanda. The girl always knew how to cheer her mother up. Then she sat down next to Logan and they started talking about school.

"Isn't Saturday the best?" Max said, walking downstairs and sitting across from Cindy.

"Yeah, for you. You don't have to go to work," Logan said.

Amanda smiled.

"Hey, I thought Saturday was your sleep-in day?" she asked.

"Well, Cindy woke me up and I smelled bacon, so I woke up," said Max.

They all started laughing. Everyone knew that Max was the king of sleeping in.

"Hey, what's this entire racket? Shut up and let me sleep," yelled Tony from upstairs.

"Oh, get up, you lazy pig!" Julia yelled.

She was cleaning Max's room for the sixth time that week. Everyone started laughing. Max resembled his grandfather.

At eight o'clock in the morning, Logan went to work and so did Tony who worked as an engineer. Amanda and Maria were not working that day.

"I'm going to the grocery store on 33rd Street. Anyone coming?" said Amanda.

Maria ran downstairs.

"I'll come," she said.

"What about breakfast?" replied Amanda.

"I'll eat it on the way out."

Amanda went upstairs with vampire speed and changed in a blink of an eye, running back downstairs.

"I love vampire speed. Don't you?" Amanda said.

"Of course," said Maria, eating bacon. She grabbed two more strips and put them in her pocket.

"Let's go," she said.

Maria loved her bacon.

They started walking down 2nd Avenue until they hit 33rd Street. Maria was gobbling her bacon while walking. People were looking at her and whispering. Amanda laughed. Maria shrugged; she did not really care. *They could look if they wanted to,* she thought.

Amanda felt someone following her. She turned around and only saw people, so she turned back and continued walking. Amanda and Maria walked into the grocery store and Amanda started looking around. She shopped at this store instead of at the grocery shop she worked in, because the former was cheaper.

Suddenly, Amanda turned around and caught sight of someone hiding behind a rack, but when she stormed over there, she found no one. First the phone call, now this. She was really confused. Amanda picked the food she wanted to buy and paid for it. She walked out and remembered. Maria! Running back inside, she grabbed Maria and walked out. They both ran back home with vampire speed.

The rest of the day was full of thought. Amanda wondered who was behind this fishy business.

"What's wrong, mom?" Cindy asked Amanda.

"Nothing, dear. I just need to think."

They were in the living room watching television. Max was foot on foot eating popcorn, watching the tube as if it was life. Cindy kept looking at her mother and started worrying. Amanda was looking at the ground, thinking.

"Mom, you know you can tell me anything," Cindy said.

"Don't worry. I just need to think," Amanda smiled and got up.

"Where are you going?" Cindy said.

"To my study," replied Amanda.

Amanda stayed in the study for the rest of the day. No one disturbed her. She went down to eat dinner, then went to sleep. The next morning, she woke up and made pancakes. She was acting normally, but everyone knew that she was still thinking about what had happened.

Sunday went by, Monday arrived. When Amanda went to work, she felt someone staring at her, but did not have a single clue who it was. Even Tony and Max felt the same thing when they went for their usual jog at six in the morning. Cindy caught someone following her to the library and Maria noticed someone hiding behind a lantern post.

The whole family was being followed. That afternoon, Amanda went once again straight to her study. She needed time to think.

"What's wrong with us? Who's following us?" Logan said.

"I don't know," replied Julia.

They were all in the living room discussing what was happening.

"Did anyone tell a human about our secret?" Tony asked.

"No. I didn't for sure. But I bet Max did," Cindy said.

Everyone looked at Max. He was eating a chicken leg. Then he stopped.

"Why are you guys looking at me? I didn't tell. I swear on this chicken leg," he said.

"I'll go talk to Amanda," said Maria, going upstairs to find her.

The door to Amanda's study was open. Maria walked in and found her sitting on the chair.

"I know why you are here, Maria. You and the others want to know what's wrong. Trust me, everything's wrong! Someone's following me. They're plotting revenge; some way, somehow. When I find out who it is, I'm going to shred them to pieces!" Amanda exclaimed with strength.

"No, I'm here because I'm fed up, too. I want to get rid of this person as much as you do. I want in," replied Maria.

A smile grew on Amanda's face.

"Tell me what to do and I'll do it, Your Highness," Maria said, bowing down.

The next day, Amanda went for a walk down Broadway. The mysterious person who was following her was wearing a hood, so no one could see his face. Maria was following the person to see what moves he was about to make. Logan was flying in the air, keeping a lookout, while Max and Cindy were in a coffee shop nearby. Tony was at work, Julia was at home.

Amanda stopped to look at the clothes in a shop window. The mysterious person also stopped by a bus stop. Amanda looked sideways and with vampire speed, ran towards the mysterious person. She grabbed him by the neck and whispered in his ear.

"Who are you?"

The person laughed and grabbed Amanda's hand. He swung her around and she crashed into the bus stop. Many people stopped what they were doing to see what was going on. Amanda bounced off the bus stop and jumped onto the person. His hood came off and Amanda snarled. He was back . . .

"YOU!" she yelled at him.

The person laughed at Amanda and pushed her off.

Then he stood up and said, "It's nice to see you, Amanda."

Dylan had an evil grin plastered all over his face.

"Did you miss me?" he continued.

"Not one bit," retorted Amanda, glaring at him.

"Heard you got married. How wonderful. Your poor husband will surely miss you . . ." Dylan said, his grin becoming wider and more evil.

"In your dreams!" Amanda retorted and sped past him.

She ran with vampire speed and Dylan was now running after her, in wolf form. *This is déjà vu,* thought Amanda. She turned around and kicked Dylan in the mouth. He whimpered and groaned once more.

Dylan climbed onto Amanda's back and she swung him off. He was thrown into a parked car.

"MY CAR!!!" someone screamed.

"Sorry!" Amanda yelled and kept running.

She wanted to tire Dylan out, but in the process, Amanda tripped over something and fell to the ground with a thump. She looked up, straight into Dylan's green eyes.

"You're coming with me," he said, grabbing her by the neck.

Amanda tried to get rid of his grip, but Dylan was too strong for her. Logan and Maria were rushing towards her. Dylan waved and the two of them vanished.

"How could they have vanished?" Julia asked.

Logan, Maria, Cindy and Max were all at home discussing what happened.

"They vanished with Merlin's Powder."

"The vanishing one? He probably stole it from him," Maria said.

"What now?" asked Max.

"We need to wait for a sign," replied Logan.

"Correct. We need to wait and see if Amanda will send us a message or something. She's strong, she might even kill him," confirmed Maria.

"But Maria, this is Dylan! He's pretty strong too and we don't know what he has in mind," Cindy said.

"We wait and see. Agreed?" Logan said.

"Agreed."

~ ~ ~ ~ ~

Amanda woke up and found herself in a dark room. She was tied to a chair.

"She just woke up, master," a man said.

"Okay. Her blood's taken, correct?" said a familiar voice.

"Yes, master."

"Where am I?" Amanda asked the two men.

They appeared a little blurry.

"It's good you woke up, Amanda," said the familiar voice.

"Dylan? Is that you? What do you want?" she said.

Amanda heard a cackling laugh. She adjusted her eyesight and saw Dylan laughing with another man behind him.

"What do I want? That's a stupid question. I want revenge! I want the throne which used to belong to my ancestors!!!" Dylan yelled at her, vehemently.

"You'll never take it, it belongs to me! And even if you do kill me, Logan would take the throne. And once the princess is born, she would," Amanda glared at him.

Dylan laughed again.

"And what if they're all dead, already?"

Amanda froze. *It couldn't be,* she thought.

She tried wiggling herself out of the ropes, but failed. Dylan's smile grew wider and even more evil. For some reason, the ropes were eating away at her flesh.

"The more you move, the more the garlic ropes will eat you away. I don't mind if you move. As long as it's painful, be my guest!" Dylan laughed and walked away.

Amanda had to destroy him once and for all.

~ ~ ~ ~ ~

"We have to do something!" Cindy told Max.

They were both in his room discussing their mother's kidnapping.

"Cindy, what are we gonna do? We have no idea where mom is," he said.

Max was on his bed playing with a plastic ball. Cindy was pacing back and forth, thinking.

"Here's a letter!" yelled Julia suddenly from downstairs.

Max jumped off the bed. Cindy and himself ran down and got squashed in the doorway.

"What does it say?" Logan asked.

They all sat down in the living room, anxious to see what the letter said.

"If you want Amanda back, come to the Statue of Liberty tonight, at eight o'clock. Go all the way to the top and that's where you'll find her," Julia read.

There was silence. No one spoke.

"I'm home! How's everyone?" Tony said, walking inside.

Julia, Logan, Maria, Cindy and Max looked at him silently.

"What? Did I say something wrong? Okay, we've gotta go," said Tony, after they explained everything to him.

"It could be a trap," Maria said.

"That's why we should prepare," replied Max.

"Now, who said you two are coming?" Logan said.

"Isn't it obvious?" replied Cindy.

"Neither of you are going. It's too risky and we don't need a bunch of kids getting in our way," Tony said.

"Come on, they're old enough," remarked Maria.

"They shouldn't go," added Julia. "And that's final."

At six o'clock that evening, Tony, Maria and Logan caught a ferry to Liberty Island. They went early because there were a lot of stairs they had to climb, to reach the top of the statue. It would take them a while. Cindy and Max were both upset. They really wanted to go and show their dad who was the boss.

"We should go," Cindy kept saying, once again in Max's bedroom, pacing.

"And how? If we go, we'd have to show ourselves and you know that's against our laws," said Max, surfing the web.

"Well, we're gonna have to break them," Cindy replied, grinning.

"What are you thinking?" Max said, scared that his sister had come up with a scheme.

"We're here. Are you sure we should do this?" Tony asked.

Maria glared at him.

"We need to do this, Tony. How dare you ask such a question, concerning your very own daughter?!" she yelled.

"He just doesn't want to go up all those stairs," Logan said, smiling.

"You two are lucky. You have vampire speed. I have to run all the way up, even in wolf form," Tony whimpered.

Logan chuckled and started running.

"You better hurry," warned Maria, dashing off.

Tony sighed and changed into a wolf. He started running upwards – a run which seemed to be the longest one of his life . . .

"If you let go, you're dead to me, Cindy," Max said.

Cindy was flying, while holding Max by his arms. Flying with Max, holding on to dear life, was hard for her. She flapped her wings and kept going, ignoring him.

Maria and Logan had already climbed the stairs and looked out at the amazing view from the top of the Statue of Liberty.

"It's very nice from up here," said Logan.

"You're right. Now, let's find Amanda and kick that twit's butt back to prison," Maria replied.

They walked around, but could not find Amanda or Dylan anywhere.

"Where are they?" wondered Logan.

Suddenly, someone grabbed him from behind and covered his mouth. Logan squirmed, but Maria noticed nothing. The person who grabbed Logan knocked him unconscious and dragged his body away. Maria turned around, but could not find Logan.

"Logan?" she said, surprised. "Logan?!"

The same thing happened to her, but she was faster. Maria punched the person in the stomach, but hurt herself instead. *This dude must be superhuman,* she thought, so she fought back and was also knocked unconscious.

When Tony reached the top, he found no one. He was confused. *Didn't they just run all the way up here? So where are they?* thought Tony. He looked around. They were nowhere to be seen. Suddenly, he felt a kick in the back and fell forwards. He turned around and saw a man as big as a boulder. Tony turned rapidly into a wolf once again and jumped on him. The man swayed Tony aside and he fell on the floor. *That hurt.* The man grabbed Tony and swung him over his shoulder. Tony started kicking and biting, until he was slammed against something hard. He fainted.

Cindy and Max were still flying when, suddenly, Max got a mind message. *Don't go to the top, they'll capture you. Go to Ellis Island to find Amanda. We are in the dungeons under the statue. Go for Amanda first.*

Max told Cindy and they argued about the message. Werewolves could send mind messages to each other, but what if it where from Dylan? Max was sure, though, that it was from their grandfather and Cindy decided to do as the message said.

Amanda was inside the same room looking at the stupid goof who was in front of her. It was the same man from before and she could tell that he was a wizard. Dylan only trusted his kind and wizards, Amanda knew. She needed to escape. *Think, Amanda, think.* Then it hit her.

"I need something to drink," she said.

"I'll tell the boss," the wizard replied, opening the door with one of his keys.

The wizard locked the door behind him and walked away. Amanda sprang into action. She started attempting to rip the thick, garlic ropes. It hurt, but she did not care. Then the door was unlocked and Dylan busted through. Amanda had not yet cut the rope completely, so she got up and hit Dylan where it hurt as he walked over to her. Still tied to the chair, Amanda similarly hit every guard who came her way. Then she started running. She could not run with her usual vampire speed as she was tied to the chair with garlic ropes.

Once she ran away from her captors, Amanda started banging the chair against the wall. At last, it broke. She slipped out of the ropes as they burned her flesh and tried running vampire speed. It was hard because she was weak. An alarm went off and Amanda tried running harder. *An exit, please. An exit!* She saw guards rushing towards her from behind. She had to make it. Amanda pushed open a door and breathed in the fresh air. She bounced off the floor and spread her wings. Suddenly, something – someone – jumped on her. She fell to the floor and hurt her back. She got up and looked at the most despicable person she knew.

"Did you think I'd let you leave so early? Amanda, you're our guest. Why leave so soon?" Dylan snarled.

Amanda snarled her fangs back at him.

"You're gonna die!" she said.

Dylan laughed with an evilness that would make you shiver.

"I NEVER DIE!"

Dylan leaped towards her and Amanda punched him in the chin. She then flew towards Dylan and kicked his ribs. He tripped her up and she fell on her butt, aching all over. He got up and towered over her.

"Say goodbye, Amanda," said Dylan, his eyes glowing with madness.

Amanda smiled: "I don't think so."

Dylan turned around and, suddenly, Max leaped on his father's back. Amanda moved out of the way and watched her son, in wolf form, beat her ex-husband. Dylan was pouring out blood. You could not tell who he was anymore.

"Mom, can I have a drink?" Cindy said, as she walked in next to her mom.

"Sure. I'll have a little too."

Amanda watched as guards started to circle around them. Her eyes went wild and she jumped on one of them. They kicked and punched until the guard ended up unconscious.

When all the guards had been beaten into unconsciousness, Max got up from on top of his father. Cindy and Amanda decided to give Dylan a piece of their minds. He was weak and neither of them pitied him.

"I hate you," Cindy said. "And if you ever think that we're not a challenge, you'd be wrong! We're your own children and you went against us!"

Dylan smiled, evilly.

"My children. Never!" he said.

"Of course, you're not our father! Logan is. He's always been," said Max.

"I sentence you to death, immediately. I'd love to do the honors," Amanda said.

"You might kill me, but this is not the last of it. The Greenburgs will come!" Dylan yelled.

Amanda ignored him.

She bent down and licked her lips. Her fangs slipped out and she drank to her heart's desire. Cindy did the same.

Once Dylan was gone, Max suggested that they go and find the others. Cindy grabbed Max like before and they flew to Liberty Island.

"Finally! Are you okay, Amanda?" Logan asked, once they were free.

"Yes, I'm fine. Come on, let's go."

Amanda smiled.

"Is he dead?" asked Tony.

"Yes," Amanda replied.

Everyone smiled.

"The magical creatures are changing. We need to remind them that Magic State is their home," Amanda said.

"But how?" asked Maria.

"I have an idea. We'll start an agency, with agents who are magical creatures. It would be worldwide. And we could help the creatures who need food or money," Cindy said.

"Excellent idea!" said Amanda, smiling.

"What should we name it?" Logan asked.

"Magic," Cindy said.

And that was the beginning of a new story.

✌ Chapter 3 ✌

Cindy Makes Magic

Five months later, things were going amazingly. Amanda had started a secret, worldwide agency and was training magical creatures as agents. She promised Cindy that when she took the throne in Magic State, she would give the agency to her daughter and make her the manager, because she was the one who had come up with the idea. Amanda also decided to leave something for her oldest son. She promised Max that he would be the vice-manager of the agency.

Both kids were very happy with this. Things were never better. But Amanda still had her people to take care of and it seemed that the time had now come. She knew that she needed one of her children, or maybe both, to find their happiness, so that, in the end, the princess of Magic State would rise and someday take her place. Amanda's children were old enough and it seemed that things needed time.

Other than Amanda's worry about the princess, the agency was going well. The magical creatures had given up on the news of Dylan's return, but it seemed that a spark of light now showed in the community of Magic State which was scattered around the world.

~ ~ ~ ~ ~

"I love the life of being rich," said Mrs Carter.

Mrs Carter was a pixie living among humans in England. Married to Mr James Carter himself, both had been very poor in their land and the main reason why, was because they had four children. But when they all came to England after the war at Magic State, gold struck through the mines and they immediately became rich.

Evan was the eldest son of the Carters: 18 years old and he had never got the chance to speak up to his parents. After him, there were the triplets: all pixies and now six years old. Evan was a werewolf like his father. He hated living in England not because he hated the country, but because his parents had changed ever since. They did not really care about their children's opinions, especially those of Evan. They were rich and did not care about most things, nowadays. Evan despised this. He wished on his lucky stars that, someday, they would all return to Magic State and live their normal, old lives.

Eating at the dinner table, Mr Carter said, "I know, right! If Amanda ever takes the throne, we are still not going back. What for? We're rich, now, among humans. Life couldn't get any better."

Evan was going to choke.

"What?" he managed to say. "How come? Life as it is, is great! But we belong in Magic State. I certainly want to go back."

Evan's parents looked at each other.

"Dear boy, in Magic State we were poor. Here, in England, we are kings. We're staying here," Mrs Carter said, a little impatiently.

"I'm going, one way or another," Evan murmured.

His mother heard him and got up.

"If you live under our roof," she started, "you will obey our rules. If not, you must go elsewhere."

Evan was shocked. His parents had really changed.

"Fine," he said and went to his room.

Mrs Carter sat down and continued eating. She knew her son would never run away. But she was wrong.

Evan was in his room, packing some clothes. He was angry and promised never to forgive his parents. He was 18 years of age and knew how to take care of himself. He wrote a note and put it on his bed. In the note, he that said he was fed up with his parents treating him like a dog, even if he was a werewolf. He added that he was leaving.

Quietly, Evan jumped out of the window and landed on the ground. He walked around the house to its front and left as quietly as possible. For a moment there, he could not believe he was actually running away from home. But he was. Evan kept walking and walking until he got tired. He found a valley and turned into a wolf, hoping no one saw him. He then snuggled up into a corner and slept as comfortably as possible.

The next morning, Evan woke up and gathered his belongings. He decided to remain in wolf form, so he carried the backpack with his mouth. He was going to head to an agency in London that was known as Magic. He was going to become an agent and go back to Magic State when the time was ready.

From Essex, Evan had a little bit of a walk and did not want to waste time. He had packed food and money, just in case. He wondered what his parents were thinking about him leaving. He did not care because he knew that he was not going back.

Truth is, the Carters were shocked when they found and read Evan's note. They sent the police on a wild search to find him, but it is not easy to find a werewolf.

After a week, Evan finally made it to London. All he had to do, now, was find the agency. His parents had given up hope. Their son was nowhere to be found, so they accepted the fact that now they only had three children.

~ ~ ~ ~ ~

"Good morning," said Amanda.

"Good morning, mom," Cindy replied, kissing her on the cheek.

"I must say, this move was the best idea, ever."

The whole family had moved to London from New York. The population in London was much smaller and the Robins family thought it was best, although they all missed New York City.

The Robins were walking through the doors of their agency, to start another day of work. The queen of England herself had been so kind as to donate money to them, to start the agency. The queen was grateful because Amanda had saved her life in a horrible fire years ago, so she was happy to help. Naturally, she knew Amanda's secret. Agents were already there, getting ready to train and help those in need.

Cindy went straight to training and so did the others. Logan was a trainer, so were Maria and Tony. Julia was the help; she loved cleaning. There was no speck of dust that she could see, that she would not clean. Meanwhile, Amanda went to her office to start the paperwork. In the afternoon, she heard panting – it sounded like a dog. *Hmm*, she thought. Amanda walked out of her office, into the hallway and saw a wolf. No one else was in the hallway except for this wolf that she noticed was really a werewolf. As if on cue, the wolf turned into an 18-year-old boy. He was tired and seemed to need water. Amanda walked back into her office and got a water bottle. She went outside, opened the bottle and gave it to the poor boy. He took it and started drinking.

"Thank you," the boy said, as he finished drinking the whole bottle.

"You're welcome, my dear. You're a werewolf right?" Amanda asked.

"Yes. And you're Queen Amanda Robins, I suppose?" he replied.

"Yes, I am. You must be tired. Come to my office and you can tell me exactly what you need," she said.

Without giving the boy a chance to speak, Amanda guided him into her office. There, he sat down across from her.

"Tell me, dear, what's your name?" she said.

"My name? My name's Evan Carter," the boy replied.

"Evan Carter. I know your parents. Nice people," Amanda commented.

"They aren't, anymore. Now they're rich and don't care about anything, lately. I'm here because I want to be an agent. Of course, I'll train first. I don't want anything to do with my family," said Evan.

"I understand. Well, sign these papers. You're 18, right?" Amanda asked.

Evan nodded and signed the papers.

"So, where are you living?" she asked.

"Nowhere, really," he said.

"I'd be more than happy to welcome you to live here at the agency, but we need to settle things with your parents."

Evan looked at the floor.

"I don't know," he said.

"You need to talk to your parents. I promise, now you've signed these papers, you're one of us, so you don't need to go back," Amanda reassured him.

"Okay. I'm not going to talk to my parents, though," replied Evan.

"Don't worry," she said and asked him for their number.

Amanda called the Carters and told them that their son was safe and sound in London. They wanted Evan to go back, but Amanda refused and said that he was now an agent in training, so there were no backsies. Evan was happy to hear Amanda sticking up for him. He never imagined himself actually talking to Her Majesty. Amanda hung up the phone.

Getting up, she said, "Come with me, we'll find you a bunk."

Evan followed her to the fourth floor. There were several rooms.

"You can choose any empty bunk you want and put your belongings in the trunk. Don't worry, no one will steal them as everyone has their own. It's best that you rest for the day. I hope to see you bright and early," she said.

"Bye," waved Evan.

Amanda departed with a smile, leaving the boy there, helpless. He chose an empty bunk and lay down comfortably. Then he closed his eyes and went to sleep.

Evan woke up hearing a lot of noise. He rose and saw teens his age walking through the door. A lot of them were looking at him and whispering. Then he saw a girl his age walk towards him.

"Hi, I'm Cindy," she said, standing in front of him.

Evan was speechless.

"You must have just joined us, right?" she asked.

"Yes," he blurted out. "My name's Evan."

"Nice to meet you. I know, it feels weird at first, being here. But you get used to it and start making friends," Cindy smiled.

Evan smiled back.

Maria walked into the room and said, "Five minutes to lights out."

"I've gotta go to sleep. See you tomorrow," added Cindy.

"Bye," Evan managed to say.

Life as an agent was going to be hard to get used to.

The next morning, Evan woke up hearing a horn. He got out of bed and went to the bathroom to change. He returned to his bed and put back his things.

"Hi, again," someone said from behind him. Evan turned around and found Cindy.

"Hi, Cindy," he said.

"Follow me to our training headquarters," she said and started walking.

Evan followed Cindy. They walked through a long hallway to a huge ground. There were Logan, Tony and Maria.

"Let's start," Logan said. "Oh. Hi, Cindy."

"Hi, dad," she said.

Evan was confused.

"He's your dad?" he asked.

"Yeah. Well, actually my stepdad. I don't like my dad, especially because of what he did to my mom," Cindy replied.

"So who's your mom? That woman over there?" Evan said, referring to Maria.

"No! She's my mom's best friend. My mom's Amanda. I thought you knew that?" Cindy said.

"Sorry, I didn't," Evan said, embarrassed.

"It's okay," replied Cindy, smiling.

~ ~ ~ ~ ~

The past days, Cindy had been trying to make Evan more comfortable. He was okay with her company. He even made good friends with Max. Amanda noticed a connection develop between Cindy and Evan. The boy started opening his heart with Cindy and they rapidly became friends. They were always together.

"Hey, Cindy. I need to tell you something," Evan said.

They were having a midnight stroll. Evan was going to tell Cindy how he really felt about her. He had really started to like her more than a friend.

"What?" said Cindy.

"I want to tell you how I really feel."

They stopped walking.

"I really like you. More than a friend. I know, we've just met but . . ."

Cindy did not let Evan continue. She kissed him. The boy was startled for a second, but he kissed her back. He found that he loved her and noticed that his life could not get any better. Evan decided that the following day, he would go and pay his parents a visit. Cindy looked at him and smiled. There was a moment of silence.

"I'm sorry if you don't feel the same way," she said.

"No, no. I do!" replied Evan with great urgency, looking at her.

Cindy smiled. They walked hand in hand towards the agency.

"I hope we wake no one up," Evan remarked.

At that moment, the lights were turned on and the pair were startled to see Amanda looking at them.

"Well, well. I was expecting to catch you two! I see that you're going out together," Amanda exclaimed.

"How do you know that?" Cindy asked.

"You're hand in hand," replied Amanda.

They both laughed and Amanda went in for a hug.

"I knew there was something special about you, the moment I saw you," she told Evan.

"Really?" he asked, surprised.

"Yes, I did. And now, I don't need to worry anymore because if everything works out, the next heir to the throne will come," replied Amanda.

"Mom!" Cindy said.

They started laughing. At that moment, Amanda's phone started to beep. She took it out and answered it.

"Hello?"

"Yes, it is I."

"Yes."

"It is safe? We can go back?" she said into the phone.

Amanda's face brightened up like a Christmas tree. She hung up the phone and could not wait to tell the news to everyone else.

❦ Chapter 4 ❦

The Lost Princess
(2023)

"Olivia, please hand me the scissors," her mom said.

Olivia took the scissors and handed them to her mother. They were in the center square of Woodland where there was going to be the market fair. Olivia's mother was going to sell the vegetables and fruit that they had planted.

~ ~ ~ ~ ~

Ever since Amanda had received that call, all the magical creatures had moved back to Magic State. Getting used to the new towns and the new life, she was happy and so were her people. Once Amanda and her people arrived, she instantly took the throne. Evan and Cindy married a year later and in a short time, they found out that Cindy was pregnant. But just before the baby was born, things went from good to bad.

Before Dylan died, he had told Amanda that the Greenburgs would rise. She had ignored him and risked her life of freedom. Greenburg (Dmitri Greenburg, called by his last name) appeared and took over, becoming the ruler of Magic State. The people fought, but it was useless. Greenburg was a wizard, one too powerful.

When their baby was born, Cindy and Evan had to give her away to an agent who promised to take care of her without Greenburg knowing, while they went to prison. Amanda too was sent to prison. She was too weak for Greenburg. But she promised her family and herself that she would not give up and that, somehow, she would find a way out.

Fifteen years passed and the people of Magic State had all become poor and sick. The only hope they had was the legend of the lost princess . . .

~ ~ ~ ~ ~

In the center square, Olivia was helping her mother work. She had never known her father. At that moment, she saw two guards walk towards her. The girl looked at them.

"Hello, miss," one guard said.

"Hello," replied Olivia, looking at the guards.

"What do you two want?"

Olivia hated every guard who was on Greenburg's side.

"You need to come with us," the other guard replied.

Olivia was startled. She had done nothing wrong.

"Excuse me? Is there something wrong?" Olivia's mother asked, jumping in.

One guard walked over to the mother and whispered something into her ear.

"Okay. Thank you," she said, bowing. "Go!" she ordered Olivia.

Olivia was speechless. What was her mother hiding? The guards grabbed her arms and started guiding the girl into a castle carriage. She tried to let go, but could not.

"Good luck!" the mother said, waving.

Olivia looked helplessly at her. *Good luck for what?*

One guard opened the door and Olivia walked in, followed by the other guards.

The carriage moved and Olivia started the conversation.

"What do you want from me? I've done nothing and you have no proof!" she exclaimed.

At that moment, the guards took off their helmets.

"Don't worry," one of them said.

He looked young for his age. The other one was old, but his face did not seem old.

"Then why am I here?" Olivia asked.

"This is going to take a while, but we have time," the old one said. "First, we're not guards. I'm Logan and this is Max. Max is your uncle and I'm your grandfather. I know it's hard to believe this, but we have time and we'll explain."

Olivia did not understand.

Then Max continued: "When you were born, Greenburg took over the land. He sent Amanda and her family to prison. You were lucky. If Greenburg knew who you really were, you'd be dead by now. Your parents are really Cindy and Evan Robins. The mother you grew up with is not really your mother, but an agent who was assigned to take care of you until the time was right."

"You're Olivia – Olivia Robins. And you're the princess of Magic State, also known as the heir to the throne after your grandmother, Amanda, herself," said Logan.

Olivia was speechless. Her mouth fell wide open and she just looked at them. What they were saying was impossible! All the stories she had heard of the lost princess were real, then! She was the princess? But why did her so-called mother not tell her about this, then? Olivia could believe what she was hearing.

"I'm the princess??" she managed to say. "And, I guess, I have to help you guys and take back the throne, right?"

"Yes!" exclaimed Max.

"Okay, I understand. But if you two are who you say you are, why aren't you in prison?" Olivia asked.

"We got out," replied Logan.

"And we're not the only two, either. Maria's broken out, as well," Max said.

At that moment, the carriage door opened and they walked out. Olivia saw nothing. They were in the forest that separated the town of Woodland from the castle.

"Up, we go!" Max said, pointing to a tree.

The tree was hollow and had a hidden door. They opened it and found a ladder. They all started climbing, closing the door behind them. At the top, were houses made of wood and ladders connecting the houses to each other.

"Well, look who we have here. It must be the princess!" a woman said and went to give Olivia a hug.

"Let go of her, Maria. She just got here," Logan said.

Maria let go of the girl. Olivia had heard of Maria. She was Amanda's best friend and was known for her heroic deeds. She was like a second Amanda. Olivia looked around her. People were coming out of their homes, to see the girl who was going to help them. They started bowing to her.

"Please, get up. I might be the princess, but that doesn't mean you have to treat me differently," Olivia said. Immediately, the people got up and went to continue doing their work.

"So, you're my family?" Olivia asked the others.

"Yes, we are. I remember seeing you when you were only a week old. Amanda was so happy to see you. Until he came," said Maria, the smile on her face fading.

"It's okay," Max said and gave Maria a hug.

"Let's get started, shall we?" Logan said.

"Get started with what?" Olivia asked.

"You're training," Logan replied.

"Okay."

Olivia shrugged. She followed Logan into a small room, while the others followed.

"Sit!" commanded Logan.

Olivia sat down on a cushion.

"Do you know how to hunt?" Logan asked.

Olivia nodded.

"I hunt a lot for my so-called mom. I even sell my killings," she replied.

"Okay. How much training do you think you need?" Logan asked again.

"I don't know."

"Okay."

Logan was thinking.

"Why don't we start with the basics and continue from there?" Max suggested.

Logan agreed. Olivia was a fast learner and the others were happy with this.

"I'm sorry, miss, but we don't have a lot of food to offer you," an old woman said.

They were around a small table in a huge room, waiting for their dinner to arrive.

"I don't mind," Olivia smiled.

"You cannot have any food. The princess needs it to set our freedom," a woman whispered to her daughter.

"But I'm hungry!" the little girl pouted.

"This is all Greenburg's fault. I wish he were dead!"

Olivia looked away from them and down at her plate. She grabbed it, stood up and walked over to the little girl.

Holding the plate out to the girl, she said, "Take this, I'm not hungry."

The girl looked at her mom, startled.

The woman said, "No, no. You need it."

"I'll be fine. Take it. I think you need it more than I do," Olivia insisted, smiling.

The girl took the plate of food and hugged Olivia. At that moment, the latter knew what she had to do – she had to kill Greenburg and bring peace to her land. She was the princess and she had a country to fight for. Nothing was going to stop her now.

A week passed and Olivia got used to things. She was training hard. She woke up bright and early, to find some wood for the fire. Olivia was not going to be a royal pain and sit there as if nothing was happening. She wanted to help her people even in the smallest ways.

She was a bit hungry. Since it was summer, there were a lot of berries around. Olivia knew which ones were poisonous and those that were not. She started picking some and eating them. At the same time, she gathered wood.

Suddenly, Olivia heard a noise. She stopped. Footsteps were coming her way. Alert, Olivia was ready for anything. She put the wood down quietly on the ground and climbed up a tree. From there, she could see what was going on below. Many agents from the MCST were laughing and chatting as they walked through the woods. They were all on Greenburg's side. Olivia could not despise them more. She knew it would be risky to come out into the open, so she stayed put. Her observations indicated to her that the agents never really cared about who was in the woods. They just walked around pretending to do their jobs.

The next day, Olivia saw many people passing through the woods. None of them knew of the secret village in the trees. It was amazing to observe people. The thing that really bugged Olivia during her observations was a boy, her age. He would always be alone in the woods, just looking around. She wanted to confront him, but knew it was a bad idea.

The day after, Olivia woke up early and did the normal scouting, trying to find wood. At that moment, she saw the boy her age come out from behind a tree.

"Oh, my gosh! You startled me," he said.

"Sorry. You startled me," replied Olivia.

"I've never seen you before. May I ask who you are?" the boy said.

Olivia knew it was not the best idea to tell just anyone who she was, in case they found out she was the princess. But he seemed to be of no harm.

"I'm Olivia. I'm a werewolf," she said.

"Clark's the name and so am I," the boy replied. "So, what are you doing here in these woods?"

"Gathering wood," said Olivia, smiling. "And you?"

"Having a walk. It's so peaceful here, I'd love to live here, rather than where I live now."

"I know. Wait. What?" she asked.

"Do you not know who I am?" he asked.

"No, I've just met you," she said.

"Oh," he murmured, looking at the ground.

"So, who are you?" asked Olivia.

"I bet you won't be too happy," Clark said.

His hazel eyes looked into Olivia's. She knew them from somewhere. They were the most beautiful eyes she had seen. He looked away.

"Tell me!" she said, walking forward.

Whoever this person was, Olivia wanted to know. She could help them.

"I can help," she pleaded again, continuing to walk forward.

Clark sat on the ground and Olivia sat down a few feet away from him.

"I'm Greenburg's son. Clark Greenburg, that's me," he said, sadly.

Olivia was startled. She was talking to the son of the one who had ruined the peace of Magic State and thrown her parents into the dungeon.

"I know what you're thinking. You're thinking that I'm like my father and that I'm as horrible. I'm not, trust me. I think my father's a madman and that he's a terrible person and a terrible father," Clark said.

Oddly, Olivia felt she could trust him. But Greenburg's son! It was too much to handle. She stood up. Clark was looking at her.

"Can I trust you?" she asked. "Please tell me 'yes.'"

Clark stood up too.

"You can. I better go, because my father would come looking and I don't want you to get hurt. I'll come back tomorrow, at this time. I hope to see you again," he said.

"Okay. I'll be here," she said and smiled.

Clark smiled back and left. Olivia went back up to the small village. She tried to act normal. She liked this guy. She did not know why, but she did and she was going to trust him. She was not going to tell him that she was the princess, but she was going to trust him.

The following day, Olivia made sure she arrived before Clark. She was first. *Good,* she thought. After a few minutes, she saw him coming.

"Hello," said Clark, happily.

"Hello."

Olivia smiled.

"Would you like to walk?" he asked.

"Sure."

They started walking. There was silence, at first.

"Tell me about you," Clark said.

"What would you like to know?" Olivia asked.

"Anything. Everything," he replied.

She smiled.

"I can't tell where I live, but I can tell you what I like to do," Olivia said.

"Okay, that's a start," he said.

"I love reading, I don't know why. I've never met my parents, so I don't know where I come from," she started.

"I'm sorry. I bet my father took them," Clark said, sadly.

"Yes, he did. I also love legends," Olivia replied.

"I do, too. My favorite one is about the magnificent Amanda Robins. My mother used to tell it to me, before she died," said Clark.

"How did she die?" Olivia asked, curious.

"My father killed her," Clark said.

A tear rolled out from his eye.

"You must have been through a lot," remarked Olivia.

"Yeah, but you get used to it. Since I live in the castle, I like to visit Amanda herself. I even sneak her some food," he said.

"Really?!" Olivia exclaimed, surprised.

She had never thought of that.

"Yes, I do. Of course, without my father knowing. I've also met Cindy and Evan. Unfortunately, Julia and Tony died. I always wanted to meet them. They died of hunger. The others escaped. My father's really angry. He says they're planning something. I hope they are," Clark said.

Olivia was happy to hear about her family.

"Why are you happy about them planning?" she asked, confused.

"I really want Magic State to go back to normal. I hate what my father's doing to this place. I always tell Amanda what's going on. She promised me that she'll get out someday. I hope so," he said, looking at the ground.

Olivia stepped in front of Clark. He looked at her.

"You really care about Magic State, right?" she asked.

"Yes. Why are you asking me this?" he said.

"If you really care, I might need your help," she said.

Clark looked at Olivia, confused.

"How?"

"Come here tonight at seven o'clock. I'll be waiting for you. We're going to help Amanda and the others escape. Please, if you're on my side, don't tell," said Olivia.

"I promise, I'll be here. I have to go. And, trust me, I'll keep my word," Clark said and left.

Olivia saw the boy leave. She went to the tree village and told Logan about her plan.

"Tonight?? Olivia, how? It's impossible!" said Logan.

"No, it's not impossible. All we have to do is work hard. It's only seven o'clock in the morning. We can make it, we have 12 hours," Olivia said.

"She has a point. We should make a battle plan and help the others escape," commented Max.

"I'll take care of that," said Olivia.

"But you don't know the castle," Maria said.

"Don't worry. I'll help the others escape and you all take care of Greenburg and his guards. You don't need to worry," Olivia reassured them.

"Okay. Let's tell the people," said Logan.

They all went outside for the big announcement.

The people agreed. It was true: they had little time, but they agreed. All at once, everyone got down to work. Olivia tried to help them all in every way she could. She liked helping others. Everyone was working hard so that this plan would be successful. They could not waste one second, time was precious.

Before leaving, they all chanted, "For Magic State and for Amanda!"

Then, they got on their horses and rode toward the castle.

Olivia stayed behind. She needed to wait for Clark. When everyone was gone, he arrived.

"I saw men on horses. What's going on?" he asked, out of breath.

"We're going to war. I need your help to free Amanda, so that she can take her place on the throne," Olivia pleaded.

Clark looked her straight in the eye.

"Of course, anything for Amanda. And for you," he said, smiling.

Little did Olivia know that Clark really cared about her. They both turned into wolf form and ran to the castle, hoping the others had managed to get in. They were in luck. The others did.

They returned to human form and Olivia told the people to follow her lead. They walked past the guards as if they were nothing. The guards had to obey Clark as he was Greenburg's son. Olivia followed him through a lot of hallways.

"Where are we?" Olivia asked.

"In the castle. Where else?" Clark smirked, teasing her.

"I mean in the castle, but where?" Olivia laughed.

"Right now, we're heading to the dungeons. Keep your voice down. We don't want anyone to hear us," Clark said.

Olivia nodded. She was worried. Was Clark using her? Did he know she was the princess? Was he fooling her? She did not know any of the answers to these questions. They kept walking. Clark stopped in front of a gargoyle. He looked both ways, then at Olivia.

"Watch this," Clark said, grabbing one of the gargoyle's horns.

He pushed it forward. The wall next to them started moving and a door slid open. Olivia was wowed. They walked into the room. The door closed and there, in front of them, was a long staircase. Clark started going down the stairs, followed by Olivia. There were a lot of stairs. At the end of all those stairs, there was a hallway.

Clark started walking through the hallway. There were prison cells with people in them. They were all hungry – so skinny, dying of hunger. Olivia could not bear to look at these people. They were probably all in there because they went against Greenburg. *How horrid is Greenburg?* she thought. At the end of the hallway, they came to another prison cell. It was dark, with only a little light peering in through a small window.

"Amanda?" Clark called. "Amanda! It's me, Clark. I've brought you a visitor."

They heard someone get up.

"How are you, my dear?" a woman said.

From the darkness, out came the beautiful woman known as Amanda Robins. Olivia was shocked. Her mouth turned into the form of an 'O.'

"You're very familiar," Amanda said, looking at Olivia.

Olivia was speechless. Was this really her grandmother?

"Please, close your mouth. That's very rude," said Amanda, smiling.

Olivia blushed and closed her mouth.

"Hello, Amanda," Clark said and bowed.

Amanda bowed back as a sign of respect.

"You don't know who I am?" Olivia asked.

"No, not at all," replied Amanda. "But I've met you before."

"I'm Olivia, your granddaughter!"

Olivia felt a tear fall from her eye.

"Olivia! You're Cindy's daughter! The little baby I never got to teach!" Amanda said, hugging the girl from behind bars.

"Wait a sec. You're the princess and you didn't tell me??" Clark said.

"Yeah, sorry. I wanted to tell you, but I needed to trust you, first. I do, though – trust you. You helped me become reunited with Amanda. Thank you!" said Olivia, hugging him.

Clark hugged her back.

"The only problem, now, is how to get out of here," Clark said, untangling Olivia from him.

"You're right," replied Olivia. "Can you bend the bars?" she asked Amanda.

"I'm cuffed. I could, but can't reach them," Amanda said.

Clark and Olivia noticed the cuffs Amanda had on her hands.

"You try," Clark told Olivia.

The girl tried bending the bars. She tried and tried. She managed to bend them enough so that she could pass through them. Both Clark and Olivia passed through the bars. Clark took one of the cuff chains in his hands. He tried to break them, but it was no use.

"Let me try," Olivia said.

She breathed in and out, then chopped the chains with her bare hands. Olivia was proud of her accomplishment.

"Thank you both, my brave ones," Amanda said, hugging them. Then she let go. "Clark, thank you. You're part of my family, from now on."

Olivia looked at Clark and smiled. The boy blushed.

"I could never . . ." he said, remembering who his father was.

"I don't mind who you come from. All I care about is that you helped my granddaughter when she needed you most. You're a hero," Amanda told him, smiling.

"Thank you."

They all passed through the bars and walked down the hallway. All the prisoners were amazed by what they saw. Her Majesty in the dungeons! Amanda, Clark and Olivia started to free the prisoners one by one.

"I forgot to tell you. Where are my parents?" Olivia asked her grandmother, anxiously.

Amanda's cheery smile faded.

"They're dead," she said.

"What??" Olivia said, startled. "How?"

"Greenburg killed them three months ago. He kept it a secret. Not even Clark knew," Amanda said with great sadness.

Olivia was going to faint. Not knowing her parents was one thing, but never being able to meet them was another.

"What's the matter?" Clark asked.

He was leading the prisoners to escape.

"My parents are dead," Olivia told him, explaining the reason why.

Clark was shocked.

"My father never told me. If I knew, I would have stopped him," Clark said, giving Olivia a hug.

Olivia felt a tear roll down from her eye.

"You'll be fine," Clark added, facing her. "You have Amanda. She'll help you."

Olivia smiled weakly. That smile turned from sadness to anger. She was going to make sure that Greenburg paid for all he had done. Amanda, Clark and Olivia climbed the stairs, while the prisoners scattered around. The trio needed to find Greenburg.

"Everything is the same, exactly how I left it," said Amanda, looking around.

She missed the castle very much. They went straight to the throne room. That is where Greenburg probably was. All three of them opened the doors and found the guards battling the people. Amanda saw

Logan, Maria and Max fighting for their lives. Amanda was so happy to see them.

"Greenburg!" she boomed.

Her voice echoed throughout the room. Everyone froze and looked at Amanda. They were all amazed. Greenburg looked slightly scared out of his wits.

"You've turned this land into a pigsty! You thought that killing my daughter and son-in-law, starving my parents to death and, most of all, starving me would ensure you'd be king forever. Don't you know who I am?" Amanda said, walking towards Greenburg determinedly.

People were making a path for her to walk through.

"Of course, I do. You're Amanda Robins. Well, guess what: there's no princess! Your dear son isn't married and your daughter is dead. I can still rule, killing you first," Greenburg growled.

"Even if you kill her, there's still me!" someone yelled.

Amanda turned and saw Olivia walking forward, head upright.

"I'm Olivia Robins, princess of Magic State," the girl declared.

Greenburg started laughing.

"Cindy never had a child," he said between laughs.

"Oh yes, she did," retorted Olivia.

Suddenly, Greenburg stopped laughing.

"Seize them!" he yelled.

Guards started running in every direction, trying to grab Amanda and Olivia. Amanda was slicing a knife through each one of them that came her way. Olivia turned into wolf form and started kicking and biting with all her strength.

"Take this!" Amanda yelled to her, throwing a small pouch in her direction.

Olivia caught the pouch in her mouth and turned back into human form. She opened the pouch and a glowing ball rose out. She had no idea what to do. Amanda was fighting off Greenburg, so she could not help Olivia. The girl grabbed the ball and closed her eyes.

"For Magic State and for freedom!" she yelled.

Olivia opened her eyes and the gleam in them showed everyone present that she was ready. She flung the glowing ball at Greenburg and he started floating, changing colors. Then he started swelling up. Suddenly, Greenburg was glowing, emitting different shades of bright light. He blew up and sparks of light fell to the ground. Everyone started cheering. The guards and the agents were confused. Amanda had suspected that all that time, they were under Greenburg's spell. She looked at her granddaughter.

"I thank you so much, my dear, but there's still a lot to learn."

Amanda hugged Olivia. The girl felt so happy.

"What was that glowing ball?" Olivia asked.

"Merlin's Killing Spell," said Amanda, smiling.

Logan, Maria and Max came over and started hugging Amanda. They were so happy to see her.

"It's time for an announcement," Amanda said.

All those present followed her towards the royal stables and Amanda asked for her royal horse, Skylark to be brought to her. Then she took hold of the horse's white strays of hair, jumped on it and rode through the forest towards Woodland. Olivia, Logan, Maria and Max followed. At that moment, Olivia remembered Clark, so she went back to find him. She found him walking through the woods, kicking some rocks.

"What are you doing?" she asked.

"Nothing," Clark said, not even looking at Olivia.

"Come with me," she replied, holding out a hand.

"Why?" he asked, looking her in the eye.

"You're part of us now. I order you to come with me!"

Olivia smiled. Clark smiled back at her and took her hand. He jumped on the horse and they rode together to Woodland. When they arrived, Amanda was greeting people. She was standing on a table, since there was no stage from where she could speak. Everyone was happy to see her.

"I would like to say, how proud I am of all you people! You've been through a lot and I'm proud you never gave up. I'd like to congratulate my husband, Logan; my best friend, Maria, and my son, Max. I'd love to introduce you to someone we thought didn't exist. Here she is: my granddaughter, the princess of Magic State, Olivia!" Amanda announced.

The crowd went wild with joy. Olivia got up onto the table and started bowing. She also saw her so-called mom there in the stand. *So that was why the mom had never told Olivia where she really came from!* Olivia smiled at this woman and waved.

The mom waved back and mouthed, "I have to go. Make me proud."

She left and Olivia felt happy.

"Most of all, I would like to introduce someone you all probably know and think is like his father, but trust me. He's not. He helped my granddaughter and, most of all, he helped me. I'd like to present to you Clark Greenburg!" continued Amanda.

Everyone started whispering. Clark walked towards them.

"What are you doing?" he asked Amanda.

"You're one of us," she replied.

Amanda pulled Clark onto the table and said, "Give him a hand, he deserves it."

The people started clapping. Clark's sad face brightened. That was where he really deserved to be. Olivia smiled at him and Clark smiled back.

"This is the new beginning for Magic State!" Amanda yelled.

And, for the present, she was right.

⚡ Chapter 5 ⚡

A New Beginning

A few weeks passed and in Magic State everything had changed. Everyone was grateful that Amanda had proclaimed and taken her rightful place as queen. She gave the people anything they needed, since Greenburg had made the taxes very high. She visited them every day. She wanted to reward the people as they had gone through a lot, so she decided to host a royal ball in a week's time. Everyone was invited.

Amanda was also teaching Olivia many skills. Logan and Maria were organizing the ball and taking care of a lot of things. Max was overseas, taking care of Magic Agency. Some magical creatures had decided to live with normal humans. This was the start of a new beginning.

"I need to talk to you, my dear, Olivia," Amanda said.

Amanda was sitting on her throne. Olivia was going to meet Clark and go hunting with him for trolls.

Clark had become Olivia's personal guard and best friend.

"Yes, Amanda. What can I do for you?" Olivia asked.

"I know it's hard without your parents, but I want you to know I'll always be here for you. You can tell me anything," Amanda said.

"I know, Amanda. Even though you're my grandmother, still, you're more than that," replied Olivia, smiling.

"Good. Where are you going?" Amanda asked.

"I'm going troll hunting with Clark. You don't mind, right?" Olivia asked.

"No, not at all. It's good you have a break," said Amanda, smiling back.

"Okay, I'll be going then."

Olivia kissed Amanda on her cheek. Then she waved and left.

"How are you?" Clark asked Olivia.

They were now in the woods that separated the castle from Woodland and the other towns. They were both on horseback, riding peacefully through the woods.

"I'm good," Olivia said.

There was silence. Olivia looked at Clark. He had gone through a lot in his youth: his father killing his mother. His father dead and his own brother had just disappeared. There was so much pain behind those eyes. It was true, Clark was different. But he must have missed his mother a lot.

"I'm sorry," Olivia said, breaking the silence.

"For what?" Clark smiled, weakly.

"Your dad is dead because of me," she said.

"No, he's not. He's dead because he was a bad person. He deserved it. I just wish my mother were here," Clark said, wistfully.

"Don't worry, Clark. She's probably smiling right now," Olivia replied, smiling gently.

Clark looked her deep in the eye and smiled. The pair started walking through the woods, hoping to hunt down a troll. They went into the town square of Woodland to check on the people. At that moment, a girl their age went running towards them.

"Hi, Clark. How's the best boyfriend in the world?" she asked, happy as joy.

"Excuse me?" asked Olivia.

"Hi, Mabel. Olivia, this is Mabel, my girlfriend," Clark said, embarrassed. He liked Olivia more than just a friend. He had tried to find Mabel and call it quits, but had failed at this. Mabel was a pixie and a very nice one at that.

"Oh, Clark never told me he had a girlfriend. Nice to meet you," said Olivia, politely.

"You're the princess! It's nice to meet you, Your Highness," Mabel said.

Olivia smiled. There was silence.

"I have to go. It was nice meeting you, Your Highness. I'll talk to you later, Clark," Mabel said, waving.

"Bye," said Clark and Olivia simultaneously. Mabel left and so did the pair.

After Clark and Olivia returned home, the princess went to her room to wash and change. She had a lesson with Amanda in half an hour. Olivia had a warm bath; the warm water felt so good against her skin. Maria was walking along when she saw Olivia in her room and went to speak with her. Olivia had changed into her clothes.

"Hello, Olivia," Maria said.

"Hi, Maria. How are the preparations coming along for the ball?" Olivia asked.

"Very good. Are you upset about something?" Maria asked, concerned.

"No, there's nothing wrong," Olivia said.

Maria gave her that look and Olivia fell for it.

"Okay," she said, sitting down on her own bed.

Maria sat down next to Olivia.

"Speak," she said.

"I really like this guy, but I don't think he's interested," Olivia said.

"Oh, my god, I knew this day would come! Tell me, who is he?" asked Maria, excited.

"You've got to promise me not to tell," replied Olivia.

"I PROMISE. Now, tell me."

Olivia told Maria the whole story.

"You like Clark!" Maria screamed like a teenager.

"Shut up! I don't want anyone to hear us," Olivia said, worried.

They kept chatting and all – and that whole time, Clark was hearing everything! Do not get him wrong, he was not spying on them. He needed to speak with Olivia, so he was waiting for her to finish chatting with Maria. Clark was excited to hear Olivia say that she liked him. He really needed to call it quits with Mabel. He ran with his all might and found Mabel. Then he told her about the end of their relationship. Mabel became very angry at him. She slapped Clark and told him not to speak to her ever again. But all that was worth it.

Clark liked Olivia and knew she was perfect for him. He went back to the castle, hoping that Amanda would not find out about his disappearance. He went straight to Olivia's room. Her lesson was in 10 more minutes, so he had to make things fast. Clark opened the door to her room and found Olivia tied up on her bed.

"Olivia! What's going on?" Clark asked.

Olivia was struggling as if she was trying to tell him something. Clark could not make out what she was trying to say. He felt someone stab him in the stomach. Suddenly, he felt faint and fell to the ground, with a puddle of blood forming around him.

~ ~ ~ ~ ~

"What happened?" Clark asked.

He opened his eyes to see Amanda next to him.

"You're fine," she said.

Clark tried getting up.

"Relax, you're wounded. Help him up," commanded Amanda.

Logan helped Clark to get up.

"Why not stay on Olivia's bed?" Logan asked.

"Okay," Amanda said.

Logan helped Clark up to a sitting position.

"Can someone please tell me what just happened?" Clark pleaded.

Amanda sat down next to him.

"Someone's kidnapped Olivia. We don't know who, but maybe you do," Amanda told him.

"I don't remember. All I saw was Olivia tied up on her bed, mumbling something. She couldn't speak. Then I just felt a lot of pain," Clark said.

"Someone stabbed you," Logan reported. "If it wasn't for Amanda coming up here when she did, you'd be dead by now."

Clark looked at Amanda, shocked.

"Thank you," he said, gratefully.

"You're welcome, my dear. We need to find Olivia. Maria's already started searching for her in the woods, with some of the agents and guards. Whoever kidnapped her couldn't have gone very far," Amanda stated.

"You're right. I guess we'll have to put the preparations for the ball on hold," Logan said.

"Of course, this is much more important," replied Amanda, getting up.

"Can I come, too?" Clark asked. "I'm Olivia's bodyguard and I was off watch. I have every right to go look for her."

"You're right, but you're hurt. Why don't you look for her in the castle, while we do a further search in some towns. Either way, she might still be in here," offered Amanda.

Clark wished he could go with them, but Amanda was right.

"Okay, you're right. Go. I'll stay here. You can count on me," he said.

Amanda smiled and said, "Thanks."

Amanda and Logan left, with Clark starting to look around the castle. The boy could not stop thinking, he was really worried about Olivia. What if she was dead? Amanda would hate him. He could never forgive himself if Olivia was dead. Something disturbed him from his thoughts – it was someone clapping behind him. He turned around to see his brother, Roderick.

"What are you doing here?" Clark asked him, coldly.

"What am I doing here? Following in the steps of my father. I won't be a traitor like you!" replied Roderick.

At that moment, Clark noticed something. Roderick must have kidnapped Olivia!

"Where's Olivia?" Clark said angrily.

"Oh, don't worry, dear brother. She's alive, for now. Until I get what I want," Roderick replied.

"What *do* you want?" Clark asked.

"What do I want? What a stupid question. I want the throne! I want every Robins to be dead!" Roderick yelled.

"You're cruel!" Clark yelled back at him. "If mom were alive, none of this would have happened."

"Mom! She got in dad's way and he got rid of her. You can't bring her back, can you?" Roderick teased, cruelly.

Clark was silent.

Then he said, "Stop the chit chat, can you? I want Olivia, so give her to me, or . . ."

Roderick cut him off.

"Or what? The old hag will send me to prison?"

Roderick started laughing with an evilness that made Clark shudder.

"I didn't know I was an old hag," someone said from behind Roderick.

Anyone could have guessed who it was. Roderick turned around and saw Amanda.

"You'll never find out where Olivia is! Kill me, but she's hidden somewhere no one knows of," Roderick said.

"I know where she is!" Clark said, suddenly. "Mom, showed me a secret room when I was young. She said that dad created it as our little secret."

Roderick glared at his brother.

"You're a traitor!" he yelled.

Roderick took a knife out of his pocket and was about to stab Clark when Amanda grabbed Roderick from his hair and lifted him up. He started squealing like a pig. She hung him up on a flag pole. Roderick was not going to be moving from there anytime soon.

"I thought you were going with Logan to search for Olivia. What are you doing here, then?" Clark asked.

"I needed to give Merlin a spell book, so I came back for it," replied Amanda. "But I found this instead. Let's go find Olivia."

Clark led the way. They found Olivia in the secret room, in the secret tower. She had not been harmed in any way.

A week went by and the ball was set. All the people attended. There were a lot of refreshments and entertainment. Clark finally told Olivia about his real feelings for her and she was delighted. Olivia loved Clark and knew that he loved her in return. Amanda congratulated them both. Her time as queen was about to end, but she was happy to leave Magic State in good hands . . .

✦ Chapter 6 ✦

Everlasting Life

People around the world found out that a huge earthquake was coming. Who would have guessed this, Amanda? Yes. Forecasters all over were saying the same thing, that the world would cease to exist and human life would die.

Amanda decided to hold a meeting live, on television, for the people at home. The meeting was going to be held at the White House in Washington, DC. No one knew about the amazing secret of magical creatures until the meeting.

It was a sunny day in July when outside the White House stood the paparazzi. In the sky, they suddenly saw a flying carpet. No, actually two! It was an amazing sight. The flying carpets stopped in their tracks and two ladies jumped off. Down they went, gently floating to the ground. The paparazzi started taking photos and asking questions as the two, young women walked inside the building. When they walked in, the president of the United States, Barack Obama, his family and all their staff greeted the two ladies and showed them into the room where the meeting was going to be held. Who were these women?

Amanda and Olivia!

The dignitaries took their seats near the bully pulpit and waited for the paparazzi to enter.

Amanda started, "People of the world, I am Amanda Robins, queen of Magic State. This is Princess Olivia Robins. We are from Magic State, a magical island that the first queen, Nancy Woodland, created many years before Christ."

At that moment, four children walked into the room.

Olivia took the stand and said, "Well, hello, young children."

"Hello," they all said together.

"I'm Olivia. How many times have your parents told you that monsters, vampires, witches, goblins and all those don't exist?"

"Many times," a girl replied.

"You know they're wrong?" Olivia asked.

The children made scared faces.

"Don't worry. They don't hurt you. I'm a vampire. I won't hurt any of you. We, magical creatures, live in Magic State. Some of us live with you humans on your land. We won't hurt you. To tell the truth, we protect you. There's a worldwide agency that my uncle takes care of. It's filled with agents who take care of humans being harmed by magical creatures. We protect you," continued Olivia.

The children were pretty shocked.

Then one boy asked, "So can we humans go to this country?"

"No, not unless Amanda says so," Olivia said.

Another boy started laughing. Olivia glared at him.

"Yeah, right!" he started. "You're making this up. Of course, they don't exist. Scientifically speaking, they are all extinct."

Olivia looked in Amanda's direction and the queen nodded.

"Oh, really," said Olivia. "I'm a vampire."

The boy laughed.

He replied, "Show me."

A spark of light instantly appeared and Olivia turned into a bat. She started flying across the room and landed on Amanda's shoulder. After a few moments, she jumped off and returned to her normal self.

"We exist, but to help you, not hurt you."

A little girl said, "How long does a magical creature grow up to?"

Amanda started speaking: "Until 40 years. Then they grow in age, but not form. You see, I'm Olivia's grandmother."

"Wow!" they started whispering among themselves.

"What do you plan to do, to stop the earthquake," the first boy said.

"Well, Olivia and I are trying to deal with the situation. It's pretty hard, I must say," replied Amanda.

The meeting went on and on as if it would never stop. The children grew increasingly shocked with every answer they got. People at home were interested in the discovery of magical creatures, but Amanda and Olivia got to the point at the end.

"We're telling you this secret because it's been going on for thousands of years and you all have a right to know," said Olivia.

"We've been planning this meeting for a long time. Remember, we're your friends, not your enemies so, please, don't go hunting for us," Amanda said.

"Now, for the next few days, everyone must stay home. You must all get ready for the earthquake, so don't go down into the cellars or underground. Other creatures are being shipped in from Magic State to help you all out until the earthquake begins," Olivia continued.

"Thank you for your time, but that's all. Good luck and wish us luck," Amanda said.

The meeting ended.

Who could have known about these creatures?! Well, now, everyone knew about them for the meeting had been broadcast live on television. Everyone around the world was saying and thinking the same thing: *How could these creatures be for real?*

~ ~ ~ ~ ~

Amanda was worrying more than usual. She needed to come up with a plan to help. The only person she could think of was her grandmother, Corrine. One afternoon, she called up her grandmother to speak with her. Amanda had been born with an unusual gift: she could speak to the dead once she called them. But Amanda rarely used this gift. She only did so when she really needed to speak with Corrine. On the whole, Amanda preferred not to speak to the dead, as she thought she would grieve if she spoke with her parents or her children.

"I'm here!" someone called.

The voice boomed throughout the ballroom. Amanda was alone, in the dark, until a heavy mist appeared and turned into the form of a woman. Amanda looked a lot like her grandmother. When she was young, they had spent much time together.

"Granny! It's me, Amanda," she replied.

"Hello, dear. How are you?" Corrine asked.

"I'm in a huge mess. There's going to be a big earthquake and I need help to control it. Many people will die and the earth will be a disaster!" Amanda exclaimed.

"I understand," her grandmother replied.

Corrine looked at the ceiling, thinking. Inside, Amanda was pleading to see if her grandmother could help.

"I can help you, but on one condition. I give you the power of the element earth to control the earthquake. But afterwards, you must sacrifice yourself and die. Only after 30 years may you return to life as immortal, with special gifts given to you by the archangels, to protect the world as a hero. What do you think, Amanda, dear?"

Amanda was torn. How could she leave everyone she loved behind? It would be painful; very painful. The queen knew, though, that she had to do this for all the living people in the world.

"I'll do it," Amanda said, firmly.

~ ~ ~ ~ ~ ~

Everyone, everywhere, was preparing for the big event – the earthquake. People were doing all they could. The big day arrived. Every street, every town, was deserted. Amanda was at Niagara Falls, waiting. Suddenly, the ground started shaking uncontrollably. It was very powerful, but Amanda was ready.

Rock upon rock started crunching together. The ground started splitting in two all over the place. Buildings started falling and noxious gases started coming out of the earth. Amanda sat on the floor and started chanting, her eyes closed. When she opened them, a ray of sunshine glowed. She rose from the ground.

"With the power of Mother Nature, I control the element of the earth," she yelled.

Amanda jumped from building to building, regaining power and rejoining the earth all over the place. It was too much to handle. After an hour battling strenuously, little by little, the ground stopped shaking. It was calming down. Finally, the earthquake stopped. People started to come out of their houses, cheering. Meanwhile, a tear fell from Amanda's eye. She clutched at her stomach. She started seeing everything blurry and was walking with a wobble. People were looking at her in surprise. Amanda fell to the ground.

~ ~ ~ ~ ~

"I'd like to say a few words," Logan said.

Everyone was gathered at the main square in Woodland, wearing black.

"Amanda was an amazing person. Everyone liked her, she was always joyful. She never yelled or was unfair. She saw good even in those who acted in a bad way. I remember the first time I met her. It was like she was a different person, back then. My daughter died because of that horrible man. I was so sad and so was Amanda. But now I feel more upset than before. I hope she rests in peace," Logan concluded.

Then he walked off the stage. Maria spoke next.

"Amanda's always been my best friend. Ever since I met her, I always knew she was special. I was accepted into her family when my parents died and I'll always appreciate everything she did for me. Amanda will be missed. I know for sure that Tony, Julia, Cindy and Evan are smiling from heaven. From now on, we have an angel looking over on us. Her name's Amanda," she said.

Maria then started crying. Max said a few words, then it was Olivia's turn.

"She was the best grandmother, ever. I never met my parents, but I know they're amazing. Amanda treated me as if I was her own daughter. I love her. I'll miss her so much," said Olivia.

Clark had a lot to say about Amanda.

"A lot of people remember my father, of course. He was horrid. Even though people thought I was like him, Amanda saw a little spark of light inside of me. She was a good friend. She helped me and I'll always appreciate everything she's done for me. Thank you, Amanda," said Clark.

Everyone present was sad. No one had any idea what was going to happen next. In a single line, the people walked to the royal cemetery where Amanda was to be buried. Once she was placed in the tomb, Amanda's eyes were closed. She was clothed in a red and black dress, with a crown on her head. She looked so beautiful and in peace. But there was still hope for Magic State. This hope was Olivia.

The following week, all the people and Amanda's remaining family and friends started making plans for the grand day when Olivia would become queen. Amanda was going to be sorely missed, but no one knew what was happening in heaven.

~ ~ ~ ~ ~

Twenty-two years passed and things were running smoothly. Olivia and Clark married and their son, Victor, had been born. Victor married Silvia a year ago and they had Emily. Eventually, Victor was killed by the people of Magic State for trying to kill his own mother. Silvia died from cancer. No one knew that Emily was the next big thing for Magic State, so she went to live in Italy with the Sisters of Saint Teresa at their convent. People thought she was just an orphan.

(2083)

Eight years later, on September 11, New Yorkers shot a beam of light into the sky to represent the Twin Towers, as they did every year in the great city. Many people would go and see them, to commemorate the day when the Towers had been knocked down. They did the same thing this time around. Suddenly, in the sky above them, people started noticing an odd beam of light. They thought it was an asteroid and many started going mad. They fled in every direction with as much speed as they could muster and tried to take cover. The beam of light, however, turned into small stars that ended up forming the figure of a person.

The stars then started flying around in ever-growing beams of light. A strong wind was felt and pieces of metal, plastic, glass and so on started gathering together. The two light beams which represented the Twin Towers were turned off and the Towers started spontaneously rebuilding themselves. The small stars continued flying around the Towers until they were completely recreated. The stars then landed in front of the Twin Towers and a bright light shined.

The stars formed the figure of a woman clothed all in white. She held her hands out and a yellow beam of light came out of them, then she started floating above the ground. A large, bright bubble formed around the Twin Towers, then disappeared. The woman landed safely on the ground. Paparazzi started crowding around her.

"Who are you?" one said.

"How did you do that?" said the other.

The woman raised her hand to signal 'stop.'

"I saved your lives 30 years ago," she said.

The reporters and paparazzi looked confused. The woman smiled and removed her bonnet. No one could believe who it was – Amanda Robins! And her hair was white. Flashes of cameras went wild.

Amanda said, "Back off!"

The reporters obeyed.

"I, Amanda Robins, am back because the world is having some hard problems right now and they're getting out of control. They chose me to return and take charge. I'm no longer a vampire now. I'm immortal, I cannot die. I was gifted by the archangels, so I have special gifts. As a present of my welcome, I've recreated the Twin Towers for you. I've also created a special bubble around them so they cannot be destroyed again. The bubble is invisible," she said.

Everyone was still shocked. Then they started cheering loudly. Amanda bowed to her people as they bowed in return. She decided to fly to Magic State to see her family.

When Amanda arrived back at Magic State, everyone had already heard the news of her return to Earth. People were cheering. Her family came running towards her.

"Amanda!!" they screamed.

They were very happy to see her. Amanda kissed Logan.

"I missed you," she said.

She hugged Max and Clark, then hugged Maria, leaving Olivia for last.

Amanda looked at Olivia.

"I've been watching you, my dear. Well done. You've proven that you're willing to take care of these people. Thank you for taking care of Magic State," Amanda told Olivia, hugging her.

"I'm so happy to see you again," Olivia whispered in her ear.

Amanda smiled and started crying. Everyone was happy.

Over the next few days, Amanda improved situations all over the world. She took care of the poor by creating houses for them and giving them food. She also had a lot of meetings with reporters to raise consciousness about the people's needs. She took care of wildfires and nature-related problems. She also visited schools all over and taught children well.

Amanda was no longer queen of Magic State, but she was someone better and proud of who she had become. Eventually, Olivia had a problem. Her son, Victor, and his wife, Silvia, died before having any children – or so Olivia thought. But Amanda was intelligent and knew better.

She told Olivia, "Leave everything in my hands."

Amanda flew to Italy. As she was now immortal, she had more power than ever. When she arrived in the city of Milan, Amanda went straight to the convent of the Sisters of Saint Teresa.

~ ~ ~ ~ ~

Emily was getting ready to sleep. She washed her teeth and went to her room. She had a large room which was empty. Emily tucked herself into bed and tried sleeping. Then she heard someone – someone calling her name: *Emily, Emily* . . .

Emily was unable to fall asleep. She got out of bed and gently opened the door. She saw someone in the hallway facing the other way. Emily got scared. She did not breathe or move a muscle.

"Emily," the person started. "I'm here to help you."

The person turned around and walked towards Emily who was still frightened. The person took off her bonnet and touched Emily's hand.

"I'm Amanda Robins," The person said.

She turned on the lights.

"Amanda Robins! What are you doing here?" Emily said.

"To help you, my dear. For the following nights, I will come to visit you and protect you. Do not be scared," replied Amanda.

"Okay," said Emily, bowing.

"Emily, you shall not bow to me. And you may call me by my name, understood?" Amanda said.

"Yes," replied Emily.

She sounded safe to talk to, this Amanda, she thought. Emily did not know Amanda closely but something made her feel like this woman was part of her life. The rest of the night, they talked and talked until Amanda had to leave.

On the following nights, Amanda visited her, as well. Emily expressed her feelings to Amanda. She told her that she had no friends at school. Children always picked on her and stole her stuff. Amanda did not like this. Emily enjoyed life with the sisters, they were kind and bought her food and clothes, but she wished that she could leave the convent more often, not just for school. Emily was also unaware that, in reality, Amanda was her great-great-grandmother.

The next day, Emily woke up as usual and got ready for school. She tried walking to school and arrived a little late. The headmistress yelled at her, but Emily kept walking to class. When she walked in, all the children stared at her and gave her dirty looks. Emily tried ignoring them as best she could, but it was hard. During that lesson, the children came up with a plan to break into pieces the bracelet that Emily wore on her hand. When the first recess was called, the kids surrounded Emily. Their captain was a girl named Martha.

"Give us your bracelet," Martha ordered Emily.

"No, my mom gave it to me," replied Emily, gripping the bracelet with her other hand.

Martha grabbed Emily's left hand – the one with the bracelet – and ripped it off her wrist. The bracelet broke and its beads scattered all over the floor.

"No!" cried Emily.

She started weeping. Martha and the other children started to laugh. At that instant, Emily became furious. She started yelling and turned into a wolf – a huge, mangy wolf. Then the wolf started roaring. The children became scared and ran away as fast as they could, but Emily ran towards Martha and grabbed her. She flung Martha to the side, then walked slowly towards her.

"Emily, stop!" someone yelled.

Everyone saw the woman and stopped what they were doing. Emily turned back into human form and crumpled to the floor. Someone started clapping.

"Good work, Emily," Amanda said. "Very good indeed. You'll be perfect."

Amanda walked around Emily, then stopped in front of Martha.

"You, why did you break Emily's bracelet?" she asked.

Martha did not reply. Amanda waited – still no answer. Amanda stepped back, closed her eyes, then put her hand out. Gold light spread around Amanda. The beads that were on the floor rose to the air and became attached to one in Amanda's hand. A large burst of light sent the children and the teachers flying all over the room. The bracelet had been reconnected. Amanda handed it back to Emily.

"Thank you, Amanda," Emily said, taking the bracelet.

Amanda nodded.

"I have an announcement to make. I speak *in lieu* of Queen Olivia of Magic State. I proclaim Emily Robins princess of Magic State," Amanda said.

Everyone gasped as they got up from the floor.

"What do you mean?" one said.

"Impossible!" said another.

Amanda smiled at Emily who looked helplessly at her.

"Emily, your parents were Victor and Silvia. Victor was my great-grandson and he was killed long ago. Silvia died from cancer. You're next in line for the throne," said Amanda.

Emily was shocked and so was everyone else.

"Wow! Really?" Emily replied.

"Yes," emphasized Amanda. "Let's go."

"Okay," Emily answered.

Amanda held out her hand and Emily took it in hers.

"Emily won't be going to this school anymore, thank you," Amanda announced.

Then she opened up her cape and took out a carpet.

"Air Amanda!" she commanded and the carpet flew open.

Amanda and Emily sat on the carpet and flew directly to Magic State. When they arrived, people were astonished to see a girl flying with Amanda. Amanda and Emily got off the flying carpet and the former put it back into her cape. Then they went to the castle.

When Olivia heard the news about Emily, she jumped for joy. Amanda had saved the day again! They held a very grand celebration. Olivia also sent a letter to the Sisters in Italy, telling them that she was going to adopt Emily. And things were never the same again . . .

🦇 Chapter 7 🦇

The Heroes
(2125)

"Hey, Fern. What's cracka lackin'?" 13-year-old Elizabeth asked her best friend, as she walked towards her the next morning.

"Nothin' much. You?" Fern replied.

"Not bad, ya know. It's the first day of school from the Easter holidays. I wish we had more," Elizabeth complained.

Fern smiled.

"Don't worry, you're not gonna die," she said.

"Of course, not. School's pathetic, it could never kill a vampire like me," Elizabeth said.

~ ~ ~ ~ ~

Around 100 years had passed and Amanda was still alive. She was still helping out as much as she could. She had kept regularly in touch with Magic State, traveled around the world and met many new people. She had also learned to control her new gifts.

Amanda had become so famous that Marvel had made movies and published comics about her. She was like Spiderman or Captain America – a hero. But she had one thing that was different than the others: she was thoroughly fascinating.

~ ~ ~ ~ ~

Elizabeth was a vampire from Magic State. She lived in Detroit, Michigan, with her parents. Fern was Elizabeth's best friend; she was human. Both girls were the same age, but they were very different from each other. That is why they were best friends. The new queen of Magic State had allowed humans to live in the state and magical creatures to live with the humans in their countries.

Elizabeth and Fern kept chatting until they arrived at school. They walked in and said 'hi' to their other friends.

"What's first period?" Fern asked Elizabeth.

"History," the latter replied.

"Yes!" They said together.

At that moment, the bell rang and the girls closed their lockers. They started walking down the hall to history class. The girls made it to Room 254 and walked in. Right after them was Mr Dave, their history teacher. Mr Dave was one of the students' favorite teachers because he was funny and never gave them homework. The students all found their seats and greeted the teacher.

"Good morning, students," said Mr Dave. "How are you all today?"

They answered with, "Good morning."

"I'm fine."

"Great."

"Not bad."

"I hate school!" said one of the students.

Mr Dave told the class to open up their textbooks to page 175. Then he started the lesson.

"Hey, Lizzie. You're a vampire," Fern said.

"Yes, I know," replied Elizabeth.

"What do you think about Amanda?" Fern asked.

"I think she was the greatest vampire ever, back in her day," Elizabeth smiled.

"Lookie here! It's the freak who sucks blood. Hey, Fern. How come she hasn't asked you for your blood, yet? What are you, O-negative?" Hank yelled.

The crowd around him laughed.

"Cut it out, Hank. For Pete's sake, I don't suck human blood. Jeez!" Elizabeth shouted, grabbing Fern's arm.

The two girls dashed down the hallway to lunch.

"I hate Hank. He's always making fun of me and embarrassing me in front of the whole school. I wish to bite his . . ." Elizabeth stopped because she did not want to offend Fern.

"Don't worry. Just ignore him and he'll eventually stop."

"Yeah, right! In my dreams . . ."

The girls grabbed the empty trays and went to buy themselves lunch.

"Are you going to the library tonight, to look up stuff for your geography project?" Elizabeth asked.

"Nah. I've got enough information. Why ask?" Fern said, as they both waited in line.

"Oh. I was just wondering if you'd like to come over to my house tomorrow, to study for our chemistry test."

"Sure, I'd love to."

Elizabeth nodded and they ordered lunch . . .

After dinner, Fern went to her room to edit an essay she had written for history class.

"Fern!" Her mother, Jackie, called. "There's someone here who'd like to speak to you."

Fern groaned and rushed downstairs. She walked into the living room and saw Amanda Robins. Her white, shining hair and yellow, magnificent eyes made Amanda look like a goddess. Fern was shocked to the core.

"Thank you, Fern, for coming downstairs to speak with me. If you don't mind, I'd like to speak to Fern privately," Amanda told Fern's mother.

"Okay." Jackie said, turning around to leave. "She didn't do anything wrong, though, right?"

"No, no. Not at all," Amanda said with a reassuring smile.

Once Fern's mother left, Amanda asked, "Fern, are you adopted?"

Fern was startled. She shook her head.

"Okay. Tomorrow's your birthday, right?" Amanda asked.

"Yeah."

"Tomorrow evening, I want you to call me," emphasized Amanda.

"Why?" Fern said.

"I need to know if something suspicious happens, tomorrow. It's for a very good cause. You won't be in trouble and I want this to be between us, okay? I don't want to worry your parents," Amanda said.

"What do you mean by suspicious?" Fern replied.

Amanda sighed.

"Anything to do with the moon or the stars. I'm not exactly sure. I have theories, but that's what I think they actually are. I'll explain everything after your phone call. Here's my number. Please, do call," Amanda said, concerned.

Fern took the paper Amanda handed her. Then Amanda smiled and left. Fern's parents were very curious to know what Amanda had wanted from Fern, but the girl said she could not tell.

The next day was Thursday and it was very exciting for Fern as it was her birthday. Finally, at 13, she was a teenager! At school, everyone wished Fern 'Happy birthday,' even Mr Dave. Fern was really happy. Her parents were going to dinner with her dad's boss, so there were no parties.

At five o'clock, Fern went over to Elizabeth's house. She thought of many reasons why Elizabeth had insisted on them studying together *tonight*, but Elizabeth had not wanted to raise her friend's hopes beforehand. Fern knocked on the front door and Elizabeth opened. The house was dark.

"HAPPY BIRTHDAY!"

The lights turned suddenly on and Fern saw all her friends from school. Her parents were there, too. Fern was surprised, but she had expected something.

At ten o'clock, Fern decided to go home. Her parents had left early and Elizabeth's parents wanted to drive Fern home, but the latter did not have a long way to go so she walked, minding her own business. The only light present was that coming from the moon. Carrying her books, Fern kept walking straight homewards.

Suddenly, she gazed up and looked at the dark blue sky. There was the moon, it seemed like it was . . . sparkling. Fern stopped walking and continued looked at the amazing moon. Somehow, she could not stop looking at it and keep walking. It was as if the moon had paralyzed her. The moon sparkled more and more and bright stars started exploding all over from it, running as fast as they could, as if they were comets.

Fern stood still, looking at them in awe. The stars were flying towards her, but she was not scared at all. She remained there, looking at them. The books fell from her hands to the ground. Fern did not bend down to pick them up; she just stayed there. Her mind was blank. She had no idea what she was doing. She could not understand why she was not moving at all.

The stars reached Fern and swirled all around her. They swirled and swirled until the girl could not feel the ground under her feet any longer. She started floating in mid-air. Her eyes were still focused on the moon and she noticed that it was a full moon. The stars continued sparkling and Fern thought she heard them chanting. A huge glow erupted and Fern found herself spinning through the air. Then she heard a huge wind blow and fell back on the ground. The stars disappeared. *Weird*, she thought.

Fern looked up at the moon again. It was still sparkling, despite everything that happened. She smiled – it seemed like the moon was winking at her. Fern grabbed her books and got up. She brushed some dust off her pants and continued walking home. Once she arrived, Fern called Amanda who instantly told the girl she wanted to meet her the next day, after eight in the evening.

"Wow, that's weird, Fern," Elizabeth said the next day during lunch.

"I know. I haven't told my parents coz I promised Amanda," replied Fern.

"I dunno. Seems like you should tell them." Elizabeth suggested.

"Why?"

"Your parents should know what's goin' on. This could be serious. You could've been abducted by aliens or something!"

"Seriously! Abducted by aliens??"

"Fern, you should tell them."

"I'm not gonna. It's probably nothing. Don't worry."

Elizabeth was very worried and Fern telling her not to worry, made her worry even more.

"Okay, then," she said. "Suit yourself."

That night at eight o'clock, Amanda returned. She was very anxious, Fern could tell.

"Come in, Amanda. Make yourself at home," said Jackie.

Fern's father, Peter, was home that night. He was a little worried about why Amanda kept going to see his daughter.

"I need everyone in the living room tonight, please. This is very important," Amanda said.

The four of them walked into the living room. Amanda looked out of the window and pulled down the shutter.

"Fern, I need you to bring what happened to you last night in front of your mind, like a video, sort of. I'll be looking into your brain – reading it, I suppose –

and will see everything. I need to make sure you're not imagining it," Amanda said.

"What happened last night?" Peter said.

"I'll see," replied Amanda.

Fern nodded and closed her eyes to concentrate. She brought what happened in front of her eyes. Fern felt weird that someone was looking inside her head.

"I can see," Amanda said after a moment.

Fern opened her eyes and sighed.

"What do you think?" Fern asked, curious.

"I was correct. But I have a question for your parents. Is Fern adopted?"

Fern was confused. *Why does she ask that?*

Peter and Jackie looked at each other with guilty, nervous looks.

"I'm adopted???" Fern yelled, bolting up from where she sat.

Her parents said nothing.

"Sit down, Fern. It's a lot to take in, but please, sit," Amanda said, calmly.

"Why do you want to know?" Peter asked, angrily.

"First, Fern should know where she really comes from. Second, she has every right to know," Amanda replied.

There were a few minutes of silence.

"Amanda, what are you doing here? Why are you asking me these questions?" Fern said.

Amanda looked Fern straight in the eye.

"Who are the parents?" Amanda asked, not looking away from Fern.

Peter froze.

"We don't know," Jackie said, looking at her husband.

"Or do you?" said Amanda, now looking at Peter.

Peter glared at Amanda.

"Her parents are Rosella and Nick," he finally said.

"Last name, please." Amanda said, smiling.

"Robins."

Fern looked with shock at Amanda.

"You're my great-grandmother?"

"Yes, dear. Now, I may explain everything there is, for you all to know," Amanda said.

She breathed in and started narrating.

"Fern, your real parents are Rosella and Nick. Nick was human. Rosella's sister, Odette, was the princess because she was the eldest. Rosella understood this and did not complain. There was peace between the two of them. You're the first-born human in the Robins family, Fern.

"Many years before either of us were born in Magic State, there ruled another family before the Robins. They were the Woodlands. Victoria Robins was good friends with the last Woodland queen, Angel. Angel had never had children, so there was no princess to inherit the throne. On her deathbed, Angel passed the throne on to Victoria who promised to take care of the land and the people.

"When Victoria was crowned queen, she made a prophecy. The first human that was born from the Robins family would be gifted with the power to control all the stars of the universe. When this human would turn 13 years of age, the moon and the stars would collide and give the child the gift. And that's what happened in your case. You were given the gift."

There was deep silence.

"So what am I, then?" Fern asked.

"You're like me in a small portion of ways. You're gifted, though you're human," said Amanda, smiling. "I'm immortal, in human form, with many gifts from the archangels."

"Why did you tell us this? Do you want Fern to be a freak?" Jackie said, very worried.

"A freak?" Amanda shouted, obviously angry. "Fern's *not* a freak. She's one of a kind, sent from the heavens! Never call her a freak! If you think she's a freak, then I suppose you think I'm a freak, too. We're alike only in a few ways. Both different. Both equal."

Jackie and Peter remained silent. Amanda calmed down and continued.

"I've been watching you very much, Fern, throughout your life from inside your head. You're a magnificent girl, I can tell. I decided to give you this news on your 13th birthday because your parents were never going to tell you and this is a gift that shouldn't be wasted. I need help, Fern. And I need your help, in particular.

"My grandmother, Corrine, had placed a curse on the aliens from the Galaxy. They're called the Galaxians. They wanted to enslave all magical creatures and take them off to the Galaxy. Corrine didn't let them. And she cursed them. The Robins family has the gift to curse people, but we don't use it too much. What happened was that the aliens were trapped in the Galaxy, until recently. They found a loophole and now they want to kill all magical creatures, take their DNA and use it against humans. They want to enslave humans and take over Earth.

"I went to see the aliens around a month ago. They're horrible, big creatures who will kill anyone or anything that stands in their path. No human or magical creature can kill them. I can. I've battled one and killed him, easily. I think you can help me with your particular gift. You control the stars. You can explode them, killing them or bursting the Galaxy. You can help save the world."

Fern was surprised. Jackie and Peter were frightened.

"No!" the latter two exclaimed together.

"Why not? I can help," said Fern.

"So you're in?" asked Amanda, excited.

"Yes!" Fern replied, similarly excited.

"No! We aren't allowing you!" Peter said.

"You're not my real parents. I'm not listening to you anymore!" Fern said.

Then she ran upstairs and started packing her bags.

"Let's go, Amanda," Fern said after five minutes.

"What? No! You can't do this," Jackie pleaded with Fern. "We love you. You're our daughter."

"You lied, both of you!" said Fern, walking out the doorway.

"I'll take care of her. Goodbye," Amanda said, leaving after Fern.

Amanda caught up with Fern in the blink of an eye.

"Do you have any idea where to go?" Amanda said, smiling.

Fern looked at her great-grandmother.

"I've no idea," she admitted.

"Grab my arm," said Amanda.

Fern grabbed Amanda's arm and they flew up together into the sky. Up and up they went. Fern was screaming her head off. Amanda flew over the town until she saw an abandoned house, then they landed safely. Fern felt like barfing. Amanda walked towards the abandoned house and opened the front door. They walked inside.

"We're staying here."

"Are you sure it's okay?" asked Fern.

"Of course. I bought this place a few years ago," Amanda said. The whole time, she was smiling. "Make yourself at home."

Amanda disappeared somewhere, while Fern went upstairs. She found a room and put her bags on the bed. Then she lay on the bed and closed her eyes.

The following day was Saturday. Fern woke up at eight o'clock. She could smell eggs and bacon – *Hmm, delicious*. Fern went downstairs and found Amanda sitting down at the dining table.

"Good morning. How was your sleep?" Amanda asked.

"Good," smiled Fern.

"I'm cooking eggs and bacon in the kitchen," Amanda said.

"If you're cooking, then why are you here? Aren't you supposed to be in the kitchen?" Fern asked.

"I can control things with my mind. At the moment, the eggs and bacon are cooking themselves because I'm controlling them."

Amanda got up from the table and walked into the kitchen. Fern followed, but stayed in the doorway. Pots and pans were flying here and there.

"That must come in handy," Fern remarked.

Amanda nodded. Once the eggs and bacon were done, two plates flew towards the cooker and the eggs and bacon floated by themselves onto the plates. An egg on each plate, with three strips of bacon. Amanda walked out of the kitchen and the plates followed, floating in mid-air. When Amanda and Fern sat down, the plates settled quietly on the table in front of them. They ate in silence. *Amanda is a good cook,* thought Fern.

Once they were done, Fern asked, "What are we gonna do today?"

"Today, we'll train until four, then go hiking," Amanda replied.

"Train?" Fern wondered.

"Of course. If you're going to help me, we need to make sure you can handle yourself to fight. You need to be in shape," Amanda said. "Follow me."

They went into the backyard and Fern saw practice dummies. Amanda first made the girl do stretches for half an hour, then they started the basics. Amanda showed Fern jujitsu and karate. At half past three in the afternoon, Fern rested. At four o'clock, they went hiking. Amanda made Fern climb trees and carry rocks. She also made her lift heavy rocks. At the end of the day, Fern was so tired that she could not walk upstairs. Despite this, Amanda still forced her to walk up to her room.

"You have to sacrifice a lot. I did," said Amanda, leaving Fern to walk upstairs.

What had she sacrificed? the girl thought.

Fern woke up the next day with a lot of pain. Amanda gave her the morning off. At six, Fern was to train for two hours. On Monday, Amanda insisted that Fern attend school as usual. She did not want Fern to tell anyone where they were living, about the Galaxians or about her unusual gift.

"Can I tell Elizabeth? She's my best friend. I deserve to tell her."

Amanda thought about it, then nodded.

"Okay. But no one else."

Fern changed her clothes, brushed her teeth, did her hair and ate breakfast. Amanda decided to take her to school. As usual, Fern grabbed Amanda's arm and they flew up together. Amanda stopped a few blocks away from the school as she did not want anyone to see her. Fern said 'goodbye' and went to school. Then she told Elizabeth everything Amanda had told her. Elizabeth was shocked and did want to believe Fern.

"You should come over tomorrow. I'll ask Amanda and see if it's okay with her," Fern told Elizabeth.

Amanda was fine with it, but Fern had training to do.

"Only an hour. Then she must go," Amanda said.

The next day, Elizabeth went over to the house. She was very excited to meet Amanda, but the latter had problems of her own to worry about.

That night, Amanda asked, "Fern, I need to do some research on what curse my grandmother used against the Galaxians. I need information. I was wondering if you knew a library that could help me."

Fern started thinking.

"My history teacher, Mr Dave, has a big library. I could ask him, maybe you could do research together. He doesn't need to know about anything. We can say we want to look for something else."

"Can you trust him?" Amanda asked.

"Yeah. He's my favorite teacher," Fern replied.

"Okay, then. Ask him if we can do some research. Do you think I should be myself or should I wear a disguise?" Amanda wondered.

"I don't think so. He's alright," Fern replied.

Amanda nodded.

~ ~ ~ ~ ~

"Mr Dave!" Fern exclaimed, after third period English.

Mr Dave stopped in his tracks and turned around.

"Hello, Fern. What can I do for you?" he asked.

Fern said, "I thought you could help me?"

It sounded like a question.

"Well, of course. What is it you need help with?"

"My great-grandmother and I need to do some research on something top secret. I suggested that we do the research in your library, if you don't mind," Fern said.

"I don't mind. Anything for my star student," replied Mr Dave.

"Okay. If we come at four o'clock today would you mind?"

"Not at all. I must be going, Fern. I have a lesson next. I'll see you later."

"Okay. Thank you."

"Anytime. Bye."

~ ~ ~ ~ ~

"This is so weird. I've never been to a teacher's house, before. What do you think it'll be like?" Fern asked Amanda, as they walked down the street to Mr Dave's.

"Umm, I don't know. Like a NORMAL house?" Amanda said, smiling.

They walked onto the front porch and knocked on the door. Mr Dave opened it with a huge smile on his face.

"Come in," he said.

They walked inside and the teacher closed the door behind them.

"Is this your great-grandmother?" Mr Dave said.

Fern nodded. Amanda was wearing a hood, so he could not see her face.

"Well, follow me. Make yourselves at home," he said, then rushed down the hall.

They followed him. Mr Dave turned a corner into a huge room.

"Whoa!" exclaimed Fern, her mouth wide open, looking at the huge library.

"Fascinating, isn't it?" commented Mr Dave.

"As you can see, I have a lot of books. That section," he said, pointing towards the south of the room, "is about Amanda Robins and Magic State. You can find a lot of information over there."

Then Mr Dave walked towards a ladder and pointed at it.

"You can use this ladder to go up," he added.

"This library's really cool. Wish I had one like this at home. I wouldn't need to go to school," Fern said.

Mr Dave smiled.

"It's never enough."

"Hey, Mr Dave. Thanks again for considering to help me," added Fern.

"Anytime. I love helping one of my star students," he said. "I'm going to make coffee. Do any of you want drinks?"

"We'll have some water, please," Fern said.

Mr Dave scurried away to make coffee. Amanda and Fern started looking at the section where there were books about Amanda and Magic State. Mr Dave walked in and gave them the drinks.

"So, what exactly are you looking for?" he asked.

"Information about any known writings, maybe," Amanda replied.

Mr Dave said he had work to do and left them to search on their own.

An Hour Later

"I've found something," Amanda said, with the widest grin on her face.

"What did you find?" said Fern.

"I've found the book that will solve all our problems!"

Amanda sat down on the sofa and opened the book. She started reading.

"Before Amanda Robins was queen of Magic State, Corrine Robins was queen," Amanda said.

"We know, we know. Skip some more," reiterated Fern.

Amanda scanned the page.

"Okay. Corrine was an amazing queen for Magic State. She was kind and respected by her people. When the Galaxians were planning to attack them, she used a gift that ran through the Robins family line to put a curse on the alien kind. This curse was ancient. It was the Trapped Curse number 23."

"What does that mean?" Fern asked.

"My grandmother used an ancient curse. That's why they found a loophole, because ancient curses aren't as secure as the curses used nowadays," Amanda said.

"How do you know all this stuff about curses?" Fern asked.

"I'm a Robins, aren't I? I learned these things back when I was your age," Amanda smiled.

"Here, I've found another book all about curses," said Fern, giving the book to Amanda. "We need to find this curse and seek an alternative."

Amanda grabbed the book and they both started searching for the curse that Corrine had used. Once they found it, they understood that there where many stronger curses that were unbreakable.

"We should use Trapped Curse number 83," Fern suggested.

"I think number 17 is stronger," replied Amanda.

"Can we use them both?"

"We can, but it would be risky. Once the curse is out, there's no turning back. If you're still in the Galaxy, you can't come back out," said Amanda, fearing the worst.

"Don't worry. We'll use them both."

~ ~ ~ ~ ~

After a week, Amanda and Fern decided to go to the Galaxy, to place the curse on the aliens. Amanda had arranged with Magic Agency to take a specialized flying carpet into space. This carpet had been made especially for space travel. It could fly as fast as lightning. Amanda and Fern would be at the Galaxy in half an hour.

"Are you ready?" Fern asked Amanda.

"I should be asking you that," said Amanda, smiling.

"Takeoff will be in five minutes," someone announced over the loudspeaker.

"Let's go."

Amanda and Fern walked down the hall towards their carpet.

"How will we breathe?" Fern asked.

"The flying carpet has an invisible bubble around it that pumps air into it. We'll be able to breathe even in space," Amanda said. "We should get aboard now."

Amanda and Fern climbed onto the flying carpet and sat until the countdown was over.

"Five, four, three, two, one," said the person over the loudspeaker.

"Blast off!" shouted Fern.

Both Amanda and Fern flew away into the sky, away and away from Earth.

"Space is extraordinary," Fern commented.

"I know," replied Amanda.

There was little conversation between the two. Fern was too busy looking around, to ask questions. Amanda looked at the alarm clock on the carpet and saw that there were five minutes left until they reached their destination.

"Fern, we're almost there. Once we arrive, we must destroy all their battle rockets and machines. If any of the Galaxians get in your way, kill them. I suggest that you practice controlling the stars until we get there. And always stay by my side. Don't go anywhere on your own unless I tell you to," warned Amanda.

"Okay. Anything else?" Fern asked.

"Always listen to my word," Amanda said, seriously.

"We're here!" Fern announced, excited.

The Galaxy was a huge, dark planet. Amanda flew silently towards it. She landed safely near a tall building.

"Where are we?" asked Fern.

"We're at the main city. This is where the captain is. Don't kill him. We must sneak in and destroy," Amanda replied.

Fern nodded. Amanda gave Fern an astronaut suit to wear. Amanda did not need one because she did not need to breathe – she was immortal, so she would not die. They hid the carpet and flew towards the building. There were many guards.

"How many are there?" Amanda asked.

"Twenty," Fern said. "Should we take them?"

"Can you handle it?" said Amanda.

Fern nodded and they ran towards the guards. These were taken aback, but tried shooting at Amanda and Fern with their weapons. Fern created and controlled stars and shot at the guards with them, whereas Amanda controlled their minds and killed them off easily. Amanda and Fern kept walking into the main building, killing everyone who stood in their path.

Once Amanda and Fern made it to the battle room, they destroyed all the weapons, machines and battle rockets they found, as well as anything else present that could be of harm. Amanda fought with all her might and protected Fern because the girl was human, unlike herself. Then an alarm suddenly went off.

"They know we're here. Let's go, quick!" Amanda yelled.

Fern ran after Amanda and they both ran out of the building.

"How do we place the curse?" asked Fern.

"We must go to the center of this planet. Go get the flying carpet. I'll meet you at the center," Amanda said, rapidly, and flew away.

She kept looking here and there while many Galaxians continued shooting at her, always missing.

When Amanda reached the center, she waited. *Fern, where are you?* she asked herself. Amanda waited until she saw a flying carpet flying her way. She noticed that on the carpet not only was there Fern, but also seven Galaxians surrounding her. Amanda flew towards them and was almost shot by a star that had been created by Fern. Amanda then landed on the carpet and turned into a ferocious lion – an ability she had. She ripped the Galaxians to pieces until she noticed more of them arriving.

"What should we do?" Fern asked, panicking.

Amanda turned back into human form. She made the flying carpet land and both Fern and herself ran towards the center of the planet. The center was a sacred place, with a huge circle and the Galaxian language written inside of it.

"We must chant," commanded Amanda. Together with Fern, she sat down inside the circle and they grabbed each other's hands.

"Hurry. More are coming!" Fern said, urgently.

Amanda closed her eyes.

"I, Amanda Robins," she chanted.

"And I, Fern Robins," the girl chipped in.

"Shall cast the Trapped Curse Number 17 to trap . . ."

"Amanda, watch out!" yelled Fern.

Amanda turned around and saw a huge Galaxian near her. She was not ready for him and he shot at her five times. Amanda fell to the ground, unconscious. Fern let go of Amanda's hand and started battling the

Galaxians that turned up. She created new stars and hit the creatures with them, exploding them to bits of flesh. One Galaxian attacked the girl from behind and grabbed Fern's hands. He tied them together with some kind of metal rope.

Fern saw red. She instantly blasted six Galaxians together with one star. Then she noticed two Galaxians taking Amanda hostage. She ran towards them and also blasted them away. Then she ran towards the flying carpet and tried dragging it towards Amanda, while exploding the other aliens to bits. Fern managed to drag the carpet to where she wanted it to be, then dragged Amanda onto it – safe and sound. Then she ran with all her strength towards the circle, not caring anymore. Fern punched, kicked and fought with all her heart.

"I, Fern Robins, cast the Trapped Curse Number 17 on the Galaxy for eternity, so that the aliens can never escape to destroy human and magical kind!" she yelled.

There was a huge burst of light and a bubble started forming around the planet. Fern ran towards the flying carpet and pressed an emergency button. Still tied up, she tried staying put on the carpet, while also attempting to make sure the unconscious Amanda also remained aboard. Galaxians were shooting relentlessly at them, but missing. Suddenly, Fern lost her balance and slipped off the flying carpet . . .

⚡ Chapter 8 ⚡

Return of the Magnificent
(2145)

"Everyone, dinner's ready!" yelled Samantha Brown.

"Coming!"

Four teenagers ran down the stairs, towards the dinner table.

"Didn't I tell you not to run down the stairs?" Samantha said.

"Mom, we're teenagers. We aren't going to listen," Jessica replied.

"What's for dinner?" asked Royal, the eldest.

"Spaghetti and meatballs," Samantha replied.

"My favorite!" Jacob exclaimed.

"Hi, honey," said Austin.

He walked into the dining room and gave his wife a kiss on the cheek. Samantha smiled. Once everyone was seated, she started handing out the large bowls of spaghetti. Then she sat down to Austin's right and they thanked the Lord for their blessed meal.

Samantha had been married to Austin for 20 years, now. They had four kids. Royal, the eldest, was 17 years of age. He looked a lot like his father, with the same brown hair and blue eyes. Jessica and Jacob were twins, 15 years old. They looked like both their parents. They had brown, straight hair like their mother, but blue eyes like their father. The youngest, Coronato, was 13 years of age. Everyone called him Cory for short. He had red hair and green-yellow eyes. He looked like neither of his parents. All six members of the Brown family were human – a normal family.

"This is delicious, mom," said Cory, smiling.

Samantha smiled back and continued eating.

The next day, everyone woke up as usual. Samantha was dressed and having breakfast.

"I've got to go, honey," Austin said.

He kissed Samantha gently on the lips and started walking out the door.

"Have a nice day," she replied.

"You, too," Austin said, closing the door behind him.

Royal and Jessica went downstairs.

"Breakfast is ready," called Samantha. "And your lunch money is on the counter."

"Thanks, mom," Royal said.

"Wait. I have two missing kids," Samantha remarked.

"They're still asleep," replied Jessica, sitting down across from her mother.

"I'll wake them up."

Samantha went upstairs to Jacob's room. She opened the door and went straight towards the curtains.

"Wake up," she said.

Jacob turned over in bed.

"Come on," he whined.

"Wake up, Jacob. Or I'll bring a bucket of water," threatened Samantha.

Jacob got out of bed lazily and went downstairs. Samantha went to Cory's room. She walked in and opened up the curtains.

"Wake up," she said once again.

"Okay," Cory groaned.

Samantha smiled and gave him a kiss.

"That's my little boy," she said and walked out of the room.

Downstairs, Samantha walked into the kitchen and saw Jacob drinking from the carton.

"Jacob! How many times do I have to tell you – no drinking milk from the carton!" Samantha exclaimed.

"I'm never drinking milk again," commented Jessica.

"School starts in five. Is Cory still not awake?" Royal said.

"He's waking up," replied Samantha.

"I'm going to change," Jacob said and ran upstairs.

"Let's go in the car, Jess," Royal suggested.

"Have a good day," Samantha said.

Jessica smiled.

"Bye."

They went outside to wait for the others.

Cory ran downstairs.

"Have the others left?" he asked.

"No. Drink your milk and eat your toast on the way," replied Samantha.

Cory drank the milk and grabbed a slice of toast.

"Bye, mom," he said, smiling and ran out the door.

"Jacob!" Samantha yelled.

Jacob ran down the stairs, grabbed a slice of toast and kept running out the door.

"Bye, mom," he yelled back.

"Put your jacket on coz you'll get a cold," the mother yelled after him, shaking her head. *Kids!*

For the rest of the day, Samantha cleaned the house. She did not work and had the house all to herself. Austin worked as an estate agent. With his paycheck, they lived like royalty. Samantha liked being alone during the day, to clear her head. She loved her kids more than anything, but needed a break from them. Their house was quite large and with four kids, it needed a lot of cleaning. At first, Samantha had disliked cleaning up. She did not know why, but she did. After a while, she had gotten used to the fact that she had to clean – no two ways about it. These days, she did not mind, but would have still preferred not having to clean at all.

After school, the kids went to their rooms to do their homework. Royal had to play music for homework, whereas Jessica needed to concentrate, so there would always be an argument. Sometimes, Cory would need help and the others had their homework to do, so Samantha would help him. The other kids would get a little jealous, sometimes, and think he was getting special treatment because he was the youngest. But Samantha treated them all equally.

Samantha cooked salad for dinner, that evening. She set the table and called the others to come down for dinner.

"But, dad, this is an opportunity of a lifetime," Royal complained.

"What's the matter?" Samantha asked.

"You're so unbelievable!" Jacob told Jessica as they walked in.

Cory walked in behind them. Everyone sat down and said the blessing.

"Dad, I don't care what you say. I'm going to," Royal said, stubbornly.

"Royal, tell me," intervened Samantha. "What's up?"

"Next week, there's an art exhibit in New York and I want to put some of my paintings in it. I've to go to New York, though. Dad thinks it's a waste of time," Royal replied.

"It is," emphasized Austin.

"I think you should put your paintings up in the art exhibit," Samantha said.

"Stop kicking me!" Jessica yelled at Jacob.

They started bickering.

"No, he's not putting any paintings in any exhibit. This is crazy! You aren't going to be an artist someday, Royal. You're going to be an accountant," Austin yelled.

Jacob and Jessica started yelling at each other, so did Austin and Royal. Cory started yelling at them all to stop yelling.

Samantha felt herself getting very angry. She clutched her fork and knife with all her strength. The room started shaking. The table and chairs, forks and knives, plates and napkins all started flying uncontrollably around the room. Samantha remained seated with the fork and knife in her hands. The kids started screaming and yelling at each other in panic. Samantha's head felt like it was going to explode. Images she had never seen before started popping into her head. A woman, so beautiful . . .

Samantha closed her eyes and started screaming at the top of her lungs. She let the fork and knife drop and got up, then started running around the room, still screaming. Then she suddenly started hitting her head on the wall. Her skin would turn white, then return to normal. Samantha threw balls of fire at the wall, but it would not burn. The fireballs left marks on the wall, but the fire would just cease to be. Everything was flying around the room. Bright lights burst out from Samantha's chest while she was still screaming. All of a sudden, a huge, white light burst into bits and Samantha fell to the floor.

~ ~ ~ ~ ~

"Where am I?" asked Samantha.

"Mom, you're gonna be alright," Jessica said.

"You're in the hospital," Royal answered.

"Honey," Austin started. "What's going on?"

Samantha closed her eyes – so many memories about her past. She had forgotten all about them, but they had come rushing back to her. She opened her eyes and gasped, then got out of bed and looked at a mirror. Upon seeing her reflection, Samantha gasped in relief. Tears started falling from her eyes.

"Mom?" Cory asked, hesitantly.

Samantha turned around.

"There's something I need to tell you all," she said.

Everyone became quiet and patiently waited to hear what Samantha had to say.

"I'm not really Samantha Brown. Before I met your father, they found me unconscious on a flying carpet, flying down from space. I was normal and human. I could not remember who I was. They carried out some tests on me, but they still could not find out who I was. So they decided to give me a new identity. I became Samantha Connor until I met your father. What happened at dinner must be a miracle and I thank the Lord that it happened."

"A miracle? Your hair is white," Jessica said.

"I know. That's because I'm Amanda Robins," replied Samantha.

"You mean, her?!" Jacob said, taking out a comic book and showing his mother the cover.

Amanda took the book and looked at the cover. There she was, in her white suit.

"Yeah. That's me," she said.

"You're crazy. Go to sleep, Samantha," Austin said.

"I'm not crazy!" Amanda boomed. "I'm Amanda Robins, from the Robins family. Gifted with powerful abilities no human or magical creature has seen, from the archangels. I woke up from the dead around 100 years ago to protect human and magical kind. I'm not crazy, I'm a hero!"

Austin became scared, seeing his wife so furious.

"Show us one of your abilities, mom!" Cory exclaimed.

Amanda calmed down and started to levitate things with her mind.

"Wow!" interjected Jacob.

Suddenly, Amanda stopped levitating things. She had read Austin's mind and he still thought all this was utterly crazy.

"Austin," she said, more calmly. "I'm Amanda Robins. Samantha Brown was a woman who forgot her past loved ones and her duties. It's a miracle I'm back."

"This isn't how I wanted things. I wanted to have a normal, *human* family. I wasn't expecting this," Austin retorted and walked out the door.

Amanda's mouth was wide open with shock. Cory walked towards his mom and hugged her. She looked down and smiled, hugging him back.

"I'm not leaving," he said.

"Me neither," added Royal.

"I'm way not leaving," Jacob commented, smiling widely.

"I'm not leaving either," Jessica said, hugging Amanda.

"Thanks, guys. I love you all. So how long have I been knocked out?" asked Amanda, as the kids let go of her.

"Three days," Royal said.

"Okay. Now, I need your help," said Amanda. "You guys aren't human."

"Whaaat?" Jessica said.

"What are we?" Jacob said, excited.

"You're all my kids, which means you guys got abilities from me. You're all immortal, with special gifts," Amanda said.

"Mom, are you serious?" Royal said, his eyes wide open.

"More serious than I can ever be," replied Amanda.

"Twenty years ago, before they found me, I was in space on a secret mission. My great-granddaughter, Fern and I were going to place a curse on the planet, Galaxy, because the aliens there were going to attack Earth. I was shot and became unconscious. I think Fern sent me to Earth to protect me, placed the curse and stayed behind."

"She must still be there!" Jessica exclaimed.

"I guess so. We need to go get her," mused Amanda.

"How?" Cory said.

"We take a flying carpet. We're immortal. We won't die from lack of air," Amanda replied.

"Cool," commented Jacob.

"But what about Cory? He's too young," said Royal.

"No, he's not. Fern was his age when she went to the Galaxy," Amanda said. "So, are you all in?"

"I'm in," Jacob said.

"Me, too," said Royal.

"I'm in," said Cory, smiling.

"Jessica?" Amanda asked.

"Oh, alright! I'm in," Jessica replied.

Amanda smiled. She snapped her fingers and twinkling stars started swirling around her feet. A pair of boots appeared on her legs and up the stars went, to her head. Once they disappeared, a beautiful, white woman was there, wearing a white, silk dress with a robe and knee-high boots.

"Wow!" said Jessica and Jacob together.

"Okay. Let's go," ordered Amanda, heading for the door.

"Wait!" Royal said. "Won't they put you back to bed, once they notice you're walking out of the hospital?"

"You wait and see," replied Amanda, smiling.

She opened the door and the others followed her out.

"Mom?" Cory said.

In the hallway, doctors and nurses were held against the walls and could not move.

"What are you doing to them?" Royal asked.

"I can control minds," Amanda said. "But not all creatures have minds. Galaxians don't."

They all kept walking down the hallway until they found an exit.

"What about dad?" Jessica said.

"He's at home. He doesn't want anything to do with me and once he finds out you're all immortal, he'll leave you, too," Amanda said, opening the car door.

"Is he serious?" Jacob said.

"Yes," Amanda said, sadly.

"Forget about dad. We don't need him. We have mom and that's enough," said Royal.

Amanda smiled. Everyone climbed into the car and she started the engine.

"Thanks. It's hard, though. Second time, my marriage has gone down the drain," commented Amanda, wistfully.

"Tell us all about your life before us," Cory said, eagerly.

"Yeah, when were you born? I don't think they are any records of your birth," Jacob said.

Again, Amanda smiled.

"I was born on 6th June, 1956. My parents were Julia and Tony. I was a vampire and heiress to the throne of Magic State. I was first married to Dylan and had two kids: Cindy and Max. Dylan wanted to kill my family and myself for the throne, but I ended up killing him instead. I got married again, to Logan. After years of slavery in prison, my granddaughter, Olivia, heiress to the throne and Cindy's daughter, saved us all. I saved Earth from being destroyed by a horrible earthquake by begging my grandmother, Corrine, to give me the gift of controlling the element earth. She could only give it to me if I sacrificed my life afterwards. I accepted. She said that after 30 years, I would rise from the dead, immortal, with special gifts to protect man and magical kind. I saved the world and, yes, I rose from the dead. The rest you know. I had a mission to stop the Galaxians, but my great-granddaughter was left behind. That's my story."

There were five minutes of silence.

"So, we have a brother and a sister?" Royal asked.

"They're dead. Everyone's dead. All I have are my great-grandchildren that keep growing in number. And then, there's you guys."

Amanda smiled.

"If we didn't exist, life would be lonely for you," Jessica said.

"Yes," replied Amanda.

"So, if you weren't shot unconscious, we wouldn't even exist," Jacob commented.

Amanda sighed.

"Yes."

There was deep silence for the rest of the way. After half an hour, the kids noticed that Amanda was not driving home, but on the highway.

"Mom, where are we going?" Cory asked.

"We're going to an old house I have in Jackson, New Jersey. Fern used to live there."

"Why are we going there? And our stuff? How will we get them?" Royal asked.

"I can answer that question," Jacob said. "Mom is levitating our things from our house to this old house in Jackson. Am I right?"

"Yes, you are," Amanda said.

"Isn't it hard to drive and levitate things at the same time?" asked Cory.

"No, not really," she answered.

And they left Connecticut and went to Jackson, New Jersey. When they arrived, Amanda smiled to herself. The house had not changed one bit.

"Isn't it weird that in the past 20 years, no one's ever gone looking for you guys?" Jessica asked.

"They did. They know I'm not dead, but that I probably went into hiding, which isn't true," Amanda said, walking into the abandoned house.

"How come they didn't recognize you, when you landed on Earth?" Jacob asked.

"I changed. That part I don't understand. I guess I lost a lot of blood, I lost my immortality. It must've come back, because I'm stronger now," Amanda guessed.

Inside the house, there were several pieces of luggage with all their stuff.

"Mom, where's your stuff?" Cory asked.

"I don't need it," Amanda replied.

"Of course, you do. You need your clothes!" Royal said.

"No, I don't. It's my nature to wear white. And I have all the white clothes I need right here," Amanda said, smiling.

She went upstairs to her room. When they heard the door close, the kids started talking among themselves.

"Can you believe this? Our mom is Amanda Robins?!" Jessica said.

"It's impossible!"

"No, it's not," Jacob said. "Amanda Robins is real, she's our mom! Can't you see the bright side of things?"

"She wants us to help her get Fern. We're all gonna be dead by noon!" continued exclaiming Jessica.

"Shut up, both of you! She can read our minds and maybe even hear us. I think we should at least try. Our mom's Amanda Robins! We should be proud even if it's a lot to take in. And besides, we're immortal! I wonder what gifts we've inherited," mused Royal.

"Is that all you guys can think about?" Cory said. "Gifts and immortality? We shouldn't use our gifts for our advantage. We should use them to help people like mom."

"Just shut up, Cory. You don't understand anything," Jessica said and ran upstairs with her luggage.

Jacob did the same.

"Don't listen to her, Cory. She's just a brat. You're right, by the way," said Royal, smiling at his younger brother.

They went upstairs and found rooms. Amanda stayed in her room for the rest of the day, while the others looked around the house. It was very old, but in good condition. At around eight o'clock in the evening, the kids were watching television in the living room, when they heard someone in the kitchen and raced there. Amanda was sitting at the dining table reading a book, with the kitchen door open. There was a lot of clanking of pots and pans.

"Hey, mom," said Cory, sitting across from Amanda.

"Hello," she replied, looking up from her book.

"What's your book about?" the boy asked.

"Astronomy," replied Amanda.

"What's for dinner?" Royal asked.

"Spaghetti," she said and smiled at Jacob. Then Amanda put her book down: "Everyone, sit down. I have a few things to say."

The rest of the kids sat down at the table, across from Amanda. Jessica did not look her in the eye.

"I heard what you all said. I read your minds," Amanda said and paused. "Jessica, you might not believe certain things about me or yourself. Jacob, you're excited to be a hero. Royal, you want things to be normal. And Cory, you don't know what you want, yet. Life isn't fair, children. It never was and it never will be. Sometimes, you just have to pick up the last, remaining pieces and continue from there, trying to build the object again. It's your choice, what all of you want. I won't force anything on you. Royal, your life might not be the way you expect it to be, but you're not a freak. You're different, but special and delicate. Your life is yours. Your life's about to take an unexpected turn and you might find happiness.

"Tomorrow, I'll carry out tests on all of you, to see what gifts you have. And from there, we will train. You'll all get used to your gifts and train into shape. If we're going into space to get Fern, we'll need all the strength we have. You're all young and young-minded, but this mission has to be carried out and I need you all."

"Why?" Jessica yelled. "Why do you need our help to get Fern? Didn't it occur to you that maybe we didn't want to go into space, to save Fern? Maybe we never wanted gifts? Maybe we didn't want immortality? Why?"

Amanda was silent.

"Dinner's ready," she said and got up.

"You aren't gonna eat?" Royal said.

"No, I'm not."

Amanda went upstairs.

The plates settled in front of the kids, filled with spaghetti and meatballs.

"Nice going, Jessica. You made mom upset," Jacob said.

"I don't care," replied Jessica.

"You've always been like dad. Stubborn and human," Royal said.

"Mom needs our help! Wouldn't you say okay to that? She's our mom, get used to it!" Cory said.

The others were startled by his outburst. They ate in silence, thinking about the previous conversation. The next morning, breakfast was on the dining table, but Amanda was not there. The kids sat down, not looking at each other. Everyone was angry at the other. When they finished eating their toast, the kids went outside. Amanda was there, waiting for them.

"I've prepared the tests. Let's begin. Royal, you may start."

Royal walked up next to his mom.

"What should I do?" he asked.

"Sit. I'll ask you a few questions. You three, go inside and watch television."

The other three did as Amanda said and went inside.

"Royal, have you ever felt something weird between yourself and the four elements?" Amanda asked.

"I don't think so," said Royal.

"Take this rock. Feel it."

He took the rock. To him it was just an ordinary rock.

"Nothing," he said.

"Okay. Drink."

He drank a little bit of water from a water bottle.

"Nothing."

Amanda nodded.

"Smell the air. Breathe in and out."

Royal did as his mother commanded. He shook his hand. Amanda turned on a candle.

"Try now," she said, smiling.

Royal looked into the fire and saw his reflection. Without noticing, he got up and a ball of fire appeared suddenly in his hand. Amanda smiled.

"I thought it would be fire," she said. "I will train you well."

Royal took other tests and seemed excited, but he could not mind control or levitate. He did not have super speed. He had ultra-strength and could duplicate himself. When his tests were over, Amanda told Royal not to tell the others anything, yet. He nodded and went inside. Next was Jacob. And after Jacob was Jessica. Jessica was still angry with Amanda, but the latter pretended not to notice. From all her kids so far, none of them had the gift to change into a lion like she did. Amanda feared that none of them would have it – until Cory.

When Amanda identified Cory with the element of water, she was impressed. He did not have any other gifts and she was anxious to know if he was the one.

"Cory, I want you to focus. Focus on the African jungle. Focus on the feeling, what it's like. Imagine yourself as a lion. Now, catch your prey," said Amanda.

Cory's eyes were closed. After a few moments, the boy turned into a lion that roared like a beast. His eyes were golden brown. Amanda smiled with satisfaction.

"Amazing, Cory. Now, turn back into a human."

Cory did as he was told. Back in human form, he smiled.

"I'm a lion?" he asked, startled.

"A half-lion, like me. Don't tell the others, yet. I'm gonna announce your gifts myself right now. Go tell them to come," said Amanda.

Cory raced inside. After a few moments, the four of them went outside and sat on the ground.

"I'm very proud of you all. You all have wonderful gifts," began Amanda. "You're probably all wondering who's got this and who's got that."

She paused, then continued: "Royal has the element of fire burning in him. He can duplicate himself and has ultra-strength. Jacob is as hard as a rock. The element of earth is deep inside him. He can read minds and control natural disasters. Jessica has the element of air inside her. She has super speed and can control minds. That can come in handy. I expected Cory to have water, because he loves swimming. He can levitate. But what amazed me was that he is a half-lion."

"A what?!" Royal asked.

"A half-lion. He can turn into a ferocious lion," Amanda said.

"Cool," Jacob remarked, smiling.

Cory blushed.

"There were a few gifts none of you got. I wasn't expecting the half-lion from any of you. Unfortunately, none of you can fly. I guess it's a rare thing," Amanda said, smiling. "I hope you're all happy with what you have."

The four kids chatted among themselves about their abnormal gifts. Amanda smiled because they were all so very excited.

"Now, all of you, go eat lunch. I'll be in my room," Amanda said and walked away.

"This is so cool," said Royal, as they walked in for lunch.

"I know. Cory, you're really lucky. Man, you can turn into a lion! I wish I got that one," Jacob said.

They all sat down and started eating.

"It's pretty cool," Cory admitted, smiling.

"I wonder why you got to be the lion?" Jessica asked.

"What's that supposed to mean?" Cory said.

"Come on. We all know how much mom treats you differently from the rest of us. It's all because she sees herself in you," Jessica retorted.

"I don't understand," Royal said.

"All of us are different from mom. We got a lot of things from dad. Cory's the only one who looks like the real Amanda Robins. Red hair, green-yellow eyes. And their personalities are alike." Jessica said, taking a bite from her salad.

"You think mom gave us these gifts? She didn't even know she was Amanda Robins, when we were all born! Jessica, why don't you just admit you're jealous of mom?" replied Cory, angrily.

"Jealous? Of mom? Why should I be jealous?"

"Because she's the most powerful and the most beautiful woman in the world – and you know it," he said. "Stop acting like a brat, Jessica, and wake up. We're part of the Robins family and we should be proud, not go against our mom."

Cory went upstairs. Jessica was quiet.

"He's right, you know. He might be younger than us, but it seems he understands much more than we expect him to," Royal said.

Jacob nodded while eating his burger. Jessica glared at them both and finished her salad. The rest of the week passed with training.

Amanda had no intention of sending the kids to school, now. Austin had called her many times on her cell phone. He texted her saying that he reported her to the government and they were tracking her down. Austin added that he wanted his kids. Amanda never sent him any messages back. Instead, she broke her phone.

Royal caught on quickly with fire bending. He was strong and powerful. Amanda saw such passion in him while training. Jacob was always excited to train. Amanda noticed commitment in him. Jessica was a problem. She did not want to train at all. The girl would not say it out loud, but she knew that her thoughts were being read by Amanda. She wanted to be human and normal, which was not fair. Cory was still young, but tried his best.

First one week passed, then two weeks. Amanda forced Jessica to train. She wanted her daughter to understand that this was now part of her life, whether she liked it or not. All the kids steadily became skilled at their gifts and now was their chance to show Amanda they were ready.

"Mom, when are we going to the Galaxy?" Jacob asked.

He really wanted to go and would ask his mom a lot. They were eating dinner.

"I don't know," said Amanda, smiling.

"Come on. Please!" he begged.

"You all think it's time," remarked Amanda.

She stopped eating and looked at her children's faces.

"Tomorrow, we're going to the Galaxy," she announced suddenly, smiling.

"Really?" said Royal.

"Yes. I think you're all ready."

Jacob started dancing.

"Stop dancing," ordered Amanda, smiling.

"I'm going to bed," Jessica said and left.

The others continued chatting together. When it was almost bedtime, Amanda went to Jessica's room. She knocked on the door.

"Come in," said Jessica.

Amanda walked in and closed the door. Jessica looked at her mother and turned her face sideways.

"You don't want to go," Amanda said.

"Can you stop reading my mind?" replied Jessica, irritated.

"No, I can't," the mother answered, smiling.

Jessica rolled her eyes.

"Jessica, I see the spirit of a fighter inside you. You're powerful, Jessica! Why stop that power and courage from doing something you know can change your world?"

Jessica remained silent.

"I'm doing this for your own good. Someday, you'll thank me," Amanda said.

Amanda walked out of Jessica's room, when something caught her attention. Royal was thinking. She knocked on his door and he let her in.

"What's up, mom?" Royal asked.

He lay down on his bed, looking at Amanda. She sat down next to him.

"I should be asking you that question," she said. "Your mind is clouded. You're thinking too much. Tell me what it is, you're thinking."

Royal looked away from his mother and sighed.

"I've been thinking a lot and I've decided being normal is so overrated," Royal said, smiling. "I want to be a hero like you, mom," he added, looking at her.

"I have a gift to sometimes see the future. I can see that everything will be okay if you try," said Amanda. Then she smiled at him.

"Thanks, mom."

Royal smiled back. Amanda got up and went to her room – the attic. She climbed up the stairs and opened her door. She went straight to the telescope and looked through the eyepiece.

"Perfect," she said.

The following day, Amanda woke up very early. In the past two weeks, she had bought a flying carpet and was fixing it during the night. She focused more and more on her plan to save Fern. In that way, the guilt she felt would not eat her alive. She woke her children up at eight o'clock and made them stretch in the backyard.

"How are we going to the Galaxy?" Cory asked.

"We're taking a flying carpet," replied Amanda.

"Are you sure that's safe? You know, they've created easy rockets to take to space," Jessica said.

"I trust flying carpets because they've been around for almost five centuries," Amanda said.

"Whatever," Jessica mumbled.

Jacob glared at his twin.

"We'll be leaving in 20 minutes. Be calm."

Amanda went inside and ran to her room. She grabbed a duffel bag and looked one last time at her walls. Many years ago, in New York, she had a study like this and the walls had been filled with the *Magic State Times*. Pictures of Logan, Maria, Cindy, Max, Olivia, her parents and so many more were on those walls. A tear fell from Amanda's eye. She missed them all. She knew she would be back, but she was scared – scared to expose herself to the world and be rejected. She needed to show the world that she was still Amanda, that Amanda Robins was still alive to help. Another tear fell from her eye. *I'm doing this for Fern,* she thought, then went to the bathroom and rubbed her face. Amanda was determined. Nothing and no one was going to stop her now. Amanda went downstairs and called her children inside.

"I have a few things to say," she said.

There was silence.

"I want you all to do as I say. If I say leave me behind, you'll leave me behind. If I say take Fern, you'll take Fern. Do everything as I say. Understood?" Amanda said, emphatically.

The kids nodded.

"Okay. Now, Jacob, you can only use your element. Royal, you need air for fire. Jessica, your element is air. And Cory, water doesn't exist on the Galaxy," Amanda instructed.

"Mom, do you know for sure if Fern's alive? If there's no air, then she might've died. She wasn't immortal," Jacob stated.

"I gave her a suit before we left. I told her it was an astronaut suit. But I had made the suit and enchanted it, so that it would always have air inside. If Fern wore it, she most likely is still alive. I can feel her," replied Amanda.

Once again, there was silence.

Then Royal said, "Let's go."

The five of them went outside and climbed onto the carpet. Amanda went in front of her children and pressed a button. A clock appeared at the back.

"Five, four," it said. "Three, two, one!"

The flying carpet blasted off into the sky, into space. It zoomed past planets and dogged under comets.

"This carpet is fast," Jacob said.

"Space is so cool," commented Cory.

"And what's cooler is that we don't need to breathe," Royal said.

Jessica glared at them all. She was not happy.

In a matter of time, they arrived at the Galaxy. Amanda frowned. It had not changed at all.

"There's a curse out on this place, I can tell. Fern must've put it on this planet. We must be careful once we get inside the Galaxy's atmosphere. It will trigger the curse and the aliens will fight us. We must fight back," Amanda said.

After a few moments, they entered the atmosphere of the Galaxy. They landed and hid the carpet. *This is déjà vu,* thought Amanda. They walked along the planet until they made it to the city.

"What now?" asked Jacob.

"We have to look for Fern," Jessica said in a matter of fact manner.

They made their way towards a huge building.

"This isn't the same building like 20 years ago," said Amanda.

They sneaked in and walked through the corridors.

"This is strange. There aren't any Galaxians," Royal said.

"Let's go outside. This isn't the place," commented Jessica.

"Who told you that?" Cory said.

"I just know it," replied Jessica, turning around.

Amanda sighed and followed her daughter. Once they walked out of the building, armies of Galaxians stood there waiting for them with guns. In the middle was a young woman tied to a post. Amanda knew who she was the moment she saw her.

"*Jukati*!" exclaimed the Galaxians.

"What did they say?" Cory asked, puzzled.

"They said 'Attack.' So let's attack!" Amanda yelled, raising her hand.

The battle began. Amanda tried to making her way towards Fern. She could not control the minds of the Galaxians as they did not have any. So she stole one of their guns and shot at them without mercy. Amanda threw them aside and, at certain times, turned into a lion. All she wanted to do was to save Fern. When Amanda finally reached her great-grandaughter, she turned back into human form and untied her. Fern fell into Amanda's arms.

"Amanda! You came back!" Fern exclaimed with great joy, hugging her. Amanda hugged Fern back.

"I couldn't fly away, I had nothing! I needed to save you. I fell from the carpet because I lost my balance. I placed the curse and fought," continued Fern.

"Don't worry. Tell me everything later. Come on, let's go," Amanda said with urgency. She signaled the others and they all ran towards the flying carpet.

"All of you, go!" Amanda commanded.

"What?! No, you're coming with us, mom," Cory said.

"Since when did you become a mom?" Fern asked.

"Long story, I'll tell you later. All of you, go! I have to strengthen the curse. I can fly, remember? You all can't. Take the carpet and go!" Amanda said, rapidly.

"You promise to come back?" Jacob said.

"I promise," replied Amanda.

She pressed a button. Fern and the kids left.

Amanda turned around and saw the Galaxians shooting at the carpet. She stopped the bullets and turned them back towards the Galaxians. Most of them died. Then Amanda flew towards the center of the planet and, like last time, she closed her eyes and chanted. Her eyes flew open and a beam of yellow light spread around her. The curse was spreading throughout the Galaxy. Amanda had to hurry and leave before it was too late. She flew away, hoping to leave this planet once and for all. Bullets flew her way. *This is déjà vu,* she thought once again.

The curse was almost complete when Amanda flew out of the atmosphere. She sighed in relief, then made loops into the air. She was so happy!

~ ~ ~ ~ ~

After two months, Fern was finally healed from some serious wounds. Elizabeth was overjoyed to see her best friend after 20 years. Jessica had apologized to her mom. She finally understood what she was made for and wanted to be a heroine. And her brothers agreed. They had decided to keep their identities hidden, so they created new ones – they became the

Immortalities. And you are probably wondering what happened to Amanda?

Amanda decided to come out to the world and explain what had happened 20 years earlier. Fern also explained some details to Amanda about what had happened on the Galaxy. Human and magical kind were more than happy with Amanda's return. Many praised Amanda, calling her the Magnificent.

Amanda was extremely happy with how things had worked out. She knew that she could not protect the world alone, so she reopened Magic Agency to train others. And so, our hero returned to her state and promised to never leave again.

Amanda learned a valuable lesson. Everything happens for a reason and in the end, you will be happy.

More Information

The Map of Magic State

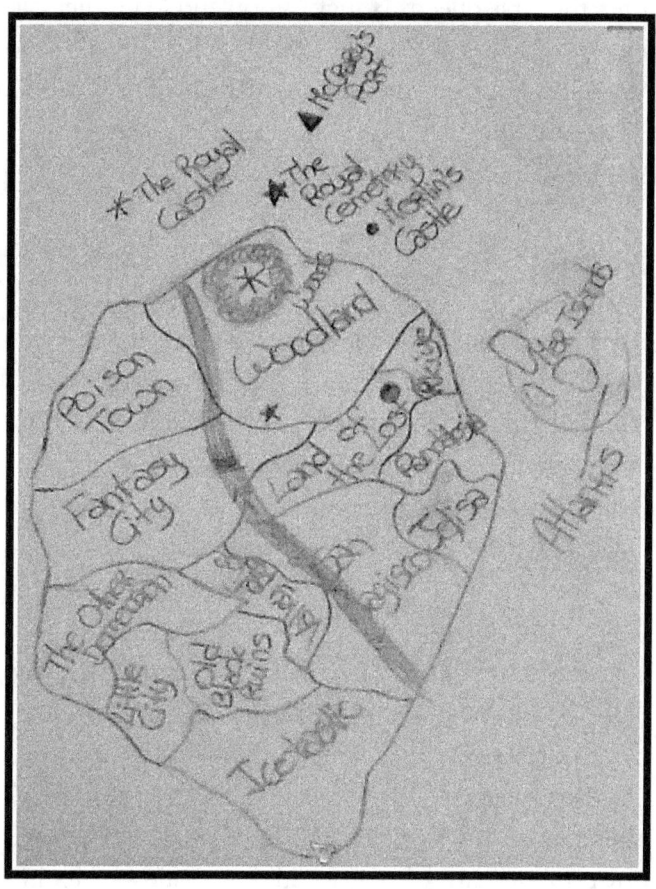

Magic State is an island north of Australia. You cannot see Magic State because it is covered with a magical bubble, to make the island invisible. In Magic State, among the population are more than 1,000,000 magical creatures. There are four main towns:

Icetastic, Poison Town, Fantasy City and San Magisco. Ten smaller towns also exist.

The city of Magic State is called Woodland, named after the first queen, Nancy Woodland. The merfolk live in the underwater city, Atlantis. There are also the Mer Islands. Each town has a school and a hospital. Of course, they live like us humans. The university of Magic State is in Poison Town.

Royalty

Even though it is the queen who rules, there is the Royal Crew that is made up of the governors of each town. Neptune is the governor of Atlantis. According to tradition, the ruler of Magic State has to be a queen. Even if the queen marries, her husband cannot be king. The queen and the princess live in the castle with their family.

The Enchanted Forest guards the castle. If the queen dies, the husband takes the throne until the princess comes of age. He is not called the king but the ruler. The first queen of Magic State was Nancy Woodland. She was half-witch, half-pixie. Merlin is a wise, powerful wizard who lives in his castle – Merlin's Castle. He has many apprentices. Queen Nancy's tomb is found at the Royal Cemetery where the royal ancestors are buried after their death.

A very important thing to remember is that when a member of the Robins family marries, the last name of the other changes to Robins. For example, when Cindy Robins married Evan, she did not change her last name like we humans do. Her last name remained that of Robins. It was Evan who changed his last name. This only happens in the Robins family because they are the Royal Family at the moment. Other magical creatures are normal like us when it comes to last names.

History

When human life form was created, other animals started to change into human form, as well. For example, bats were changed to half-human and became vampires. At first, they could not control their changing between the two forms. These creatures were being killed, so they ran off to the island now known as Magic State. Nancy Woodland was the founder of this land, so she was elected queen. It is from there that the tradition started that only a queen may rule. They even named the island 'Woodland' but it changed through time.

Special Gifts

The Robins family had the special gift of being able to place curses on people, things, creatures and basically anything. This gift was mostly hidden and remained a secret within the Robins family. When Amanda was a vampire, she had the extraordinary gift of being able to speak to dead people. But she did use this gift very much because of grief. The gift died away once she rose from the dead.

When Amanda became immortal, she was given many other, special gifts by the archangels. Here is the list of the gifts she was granted:

- ❖ Read and control minds
- ❖ Ultra strength
- ❖ Levitate things with her mind
- ❖ Super speed
- ❖ Control the four elements
- ❖ Fly
- ❖ Control natural disasters
- ❖ Duplicate herself
- ❖ Turn into a lion
- ❖ See the future sometimes
- ❖ Extra knowledge

and many more gifts which remain undiscovered.

⚡ THE END ⚡

About the Author

Corrine Annette Zahra is 14 years of age and from New York City, United States of America. Born of Maltese parents, she presently lives in Nadur, Gozo, in the Maltese Islands. She attends the Agius de Soldanis Gozo College Girls Secondary School.

In 2013, Corrine was a dual book winner in the Gozo Live Book Fair Competition, coming first in both the short story and play categories with *The Vampire Slayer* and *Back in Time* respectively. Corrine's hobbies are reading and writing.

Corrine Annette Zahra can be found online at:
- ❖ Wattpad: http://wattpad.com/user/USAgirl4eva
- ❖ Facebook:
  http://facebook.com/thelegendofamandarobins

- ❖ Goodreads:
  https://www.goodreads.com/user/show/266 83605-corrine-annette-zahra
- ❖ Twitter:
  http://twitter.com/@randompersonCAZ
- ❖ Google+:
  https://plus.google.com/u/0/100943935223 657748799/posts
- ❖ LinkedIn:
  https://www.linkedin.com/in/corrineannette zahra
- ❖ Pinterest:
  http://www.pinterest.com/corrineannettez/

Selected FARAXA Publications

Stories My Parents Told Me – Tales of Growing Up in Wartime Malta by Rupert C. Grech is a collection of seven short stories based on actual events during World War II on the Mediterranean island nation of Malta. The stories describe a difficult time for children and their families where survival was paramount and family ties were what sustained them. These stories are interspersed with snippets of history, factual details and descriptions which establish a setting for tales which are, at times, emotionally moving and, at other times, bring a smile to your face. These stories also describe a culture of a time past for a deeply religious and frugal people.

Ricasoli Soldier – A Novel Inspired by True Events by Joe Scicluna presents the story of Leo who left his native Sicily in 1806, to serve in the British Army in the Mediterranean island of Malta. All Leo had were the dreams and ambitions of youth. He wanted to become a professional soldier to be able to serve his country. Based at Fort Ricasoli, he forged new  friendships and fell in love with Lisa, a village girl from Kalkara, Malta. But his hopes, his dreams and his ambitions turned into a terrifying ordeal and a desperate struggle to stay alive.

Bormla – A Struggling Community by JosAnn Cutajar, Ph.D., is a landmark, mixed methods study in which is presented the current situation of the people of this impoverished, historical, European city in the Maltese Islands. Measures that can be taken by the community, the nation and politicians are also presented, to heal the social ills of this city. Research study after research study has shown that communities living in places stigmatized by policy makers, the media and the general population, develop coping skills to acquire alternative resources for their social well-being. In Maltese society, resources are often deployed by policy and decision makers who remain not cognizant of the differential needs of communities living in different places. Policies which look neutral on paper are anything but neutral when applied. In this study, Cutajar gives voice to the unheard people of Bormla, brings their needs to the forefront and provides effective resources for change.

Popular Operas in the Maltese Islands by Tony C. Cutajar presents the 20 most popular operas in the Maltese islands, from the time they started being produced until the present time. Almost all of them are sentimental or tragic, lyric operas. Interesting details about each of the operas and their composers are provided, together with summaries of their plots and interactive links to audio-video selections of the best arias. The beauty of operas is truly appreciated when they are seen on stage, enhanced by music which remains timeless.

The Battle Roar of Silence – Foucault and the Carceral System by Meinrad Calleja explores the philosophical rationales sustaining morality, law, punishment and the carceral system as part of the discourse of globalisation. This text attempts to desacralize the foundations of this globalisation discourse by drawing upon Foucault's 'archaeological' and 'genealogical' study of institutions, knowledge, discourse and power. This is an interdisciplinary study fusing aspects of sociology and psychoanalysis within a philosophical framework to tender a politically-charged critique of the contemporary modes of domination and power.

Pseudo-scientific pathologies born from carceral discourses are disseminated and reproduced as an integral feature of the contemporary political culture and its dominant ideology. The proliferation of these pathologies often serves as a reference point against which various categories, identities and values are registered, classified and rendered plausible.

In *The Battle Roar of Silence*, Calleja attempts to deconstruct the very plausibility structures that sustain these ideological constructs. The text correlates the carceral system discourse to political, social and economic antagonisms that have eroded human rights, democracy and freedom. Consumers of this discourse suffer the negative features of this despotic order in silence. Indeed, this text articulates the battle roar of silence.

The Philosophy of Desert Metaphors in Ibrahim al-Koni – The Bleeding of the Stone by Meinrad Calleja explores one of the works of Ibrahim al-Koni, a Tuareg by birth and who is no longer considered simply an emerging author. Al-Koni's works have earned him international repute and prestigious academic recognition. Themed primarily around a desert context, his novels have been categorized as post-modern, polyphonic, magical or socialist realism, and Sufi fabula. This book takes a close look at one of al-Koni's works – *The Bleeding of the Stone* – and attempts to prise out philosophical reflections concealed in the text. In it the desert provides a landscape rich in allusions while metaphors allow readers to engage in creative interpretation.

The Adventures of Joe Fenek by Graham Bayes comprise six short stories about Joe Fenek – Joe the Rabbit. The stories are Joe Fenek's lucky escape, Joe Fenek's good deed, Joe Fenek and the monster, Joe Fenek goes to the feast, Joe

Fenek and the chocolate, Joe Fenek and the ghost. Meet Joe and his animal friends Jimmy the rat, Digger the shrew, Tony the rat, Horace the horse, Mario the mouse and Spikey the hedgehog, all of which share in Joe's adventures around the Mediterranean islands of Malta and Gozo. Enjoy all the ways these animal buddies devise to get out of endlessly tricky situations, some of which can also be very sticky . . .

www.ingramcontent.com/pod-product-compliance
Lightning Source LLC
Chambersburg PA
CBHW060926180626
46817CB00004B/1407